TRUE *Blue*

**Center Point
Large Print**

Also by Diana Palmer and available from Center Point Large Print:

Diamond in the Rough
The Maverick
Noelle
Will of Steel

DIANA PALMER

TRUE *Blue*

CENTER POINT LARGE PRINT
THORNDIKE, MAINE

This Center Point Large Print edition is published
in the year 2012 by arrangement with
Harlequin Books S.A.

The text of this Large Print edition is unabridged.
In other aspects, this book may
vary from the original edition.
Printed in the United States of America
on permanent paper.
Set in 16-point Times New Roman type.

ISBN: 978-1-61173-296-2

Library of Congress Cataloging-in-Publication Data

Palmer, Diana.
True blue / Diana Palmer. — Large print ed.
p. cm. — (Center Point large print edition)
ISBN 978-1-61173-296-2 (library binding : alk. paper)
1. Large type books. I. Title.
PS3566.A513T77 2012
813′.54—dc23
                                        2011041785

Dear Reader,

For many years, San Antonio detective sergeant Rick Marquez has wandered through the pages of my books. Even when he wasn't featured in the novel, he's made cameo appearances. You might notice that I like him, a lot.

He was inspired by one of the greatest soccer players who ever walked onto a playing field: Rafa Marquez, who captained the Mexico soccer team and played for Barcelona for many years. I don't follow other sports, but I love soccer.

There's also a sweet, and rather stumbly, uncoordinated sort of woman named Gwendolyn who is a newcomer in Rick's department. She has a stated background, but it's still rather mysterious. Rick is always picking her up when she falls and tidying her up. He thinks of her as a nuisance. But that may change.

I love people in law enforcement, did you notice? That's why so many of my books deal with the subject. My husband's best friend, Bill, is in law enforcement. I hasten to add that I only consult with him on legal definitions and precedents, not on actual cases. He never speaks of those. A kinder, nicer man has never been born. His wife, Harriett, is also a sweetie, and his kids, Megan and William, too.

Our next-door neighbor, Gene, now deceased, was a police officer in Clarkesville, Georgia, when I was a reporter. I used to hang out in the police station, and in the courthouse with the civil defense guys (yes, it's GEMA now, I know) whose very capable boss was Barry Church, now retired. The 911 operation came along after I left, but Cindy in Pennsylvania brought me up to speed on that amazing profession.

I know a lot about all these areas because of the kind people I've met over the years. I admire them so much. So this book is a little recognition of the selfless, wonderful job they do. I am your biggest fan. And the biggest fan of my exceptionally kind readers, who make my life so rich with their presence.

Thank you as always for the years of support, for the prayers, the happy thoughts, the kind emails.

Much love to you from,
Diana Palmer

CHAPTER 1

"We could lose the case," San Antonio Detective Sergeant Rick Marquez muttered as he glared at one of the newest detectives on his squad.

"I'm really sorry," Gwendolyn Cassaway said, wincing. "I tripped. It was an accident."

He stared at her through narrowed dark eyes, his sensual lips compressed. "You tripped because you're nearsighted and you won't wear glasses." Personally, he didn't think the lack of them did anything for her, if vanity was the issue. She had a pleasant face, and an exquisite complexion, but she was no raving beauty. Her finest feature was her wealth of thick platinum-blond hair that she wore in a high bun on top of her head. She never wore it down.

"Glasses get in my way and I can't ever get them clean enough," she muttered. "That coating just causes smears unless you use the proper cleaning materials. And I can't ever find them," she said defensively.

He drew in a long, exasperated breath and perched on the edge of the desk in his office. In the posture, his .45 Colt ACP in its distinctive leather holster was displayed next to his badge on his belt. So were his powerful legs, and to their best advantage. He was tall and muscular, without it being obvious. He had a light olive complexion and thick long black hair that he wore in a ponytail. He was very attractive, but he couldn't ever seem to wind up with a serious girlfriend. Women found him useful as a sympathetic shoulder to cry on over their true loves. One woman refused to date him when she realized that he wore his pistol even off duty. He'd tried to explain that it was a necessary thing, but it hadn't given him any points with her. He went to the opera, which he loved, all alone. He went everywhere alone. He was almost thirty-one, and lonelier than ever. It made him irritable.

And here was Gwen making it all worse, messing up his crime scene, threatening the delicate chain of evidence that could lead to a conviction in a complex murder.

A college freshman, pretty and blonde, had been brutally assaulted and killed. They had no suspects and trace evidence was very sketchy already. Gwen had almost contaminated the scene by stepping too close to a blood smear.

He was not in a good mood. He was hungry. He was going to be late for lunch, because he had to chew her out. If he didn't, the lieutenant surely

8

would, and Cal Hollister was even meaner than Marquez.

"You could also lose your job," Marquez pointed out. "You're new in the department."

She grimaced. "I know." She shrugged. "I guess I could go back to the Atlanta P.D. if I had to," she said with grim resignation. She looked at him with pale green eyes that were almost translucent. He'd never seen eyes that color.

"You just have to be more careful, Cassaway," he cautioned.

"Yes, sir. I'll do my best."

He tried not to look at the T-shirt she was wearing under a lightweight denim jacket with her jeans. It was unseasonably warm for November but a jacket felt good against the morning chill.

On her T-shirt was a picture of a little green alien, the sort sold in novelty shops, with a legend that read, Have You Seen My Spaceship? He averted his eyes and tried not to grin.

She tugged her jacket closer. "Sorry. But they don't have any regulations against T-shirts here, do they?"

"If the lieutenant sees that one, you'll find out," he said.

She sighed. "I'll try to conform. It's just that I come from a very weird family. My mother worked for the FBI. My father was, uh, in the military. My brother is . . ." She hesitated and swallowed. "My brother *was* in military intelligence."

9

He frowned. "Deceased?"

She nodded. She still couldn't talk about it. The pain was too fresh.

"Sorry," he said stiffly.

She shifted. "Larry died very bravely during a covert ops mission in the Middle East. But he was my only sibling. It's hard to talk about."

"I can understand that." He stood up, glancing at the military watch he wore on his left wrist. "Time for lunch."

"Oh, I have other plans . . ." she began quickly.

He glared at her. "It was a remark, not an invitation. I don't date colleagues," he said very curtly.

She blushed all the way down to her throat. She swallowed and stood taller. "Sorry. I was . . . I meant . . . that is . . ."

He waved the excuses away. "We'll talk about this some more later. Meanwhile, please do something about your vision. You can't investigate a crime scene you can't see!"

She nodded. "Yes, sir. Absolutely."

He opened the door and let her go out first, noticing absently that her head only came up to his shoulder and that she smelled like spring roses, the pink ones that grew in his mother's garden down in Jacobsville. It was an elusive, very faint fragrance. He approved. Some women who worked in the office seemed to bathe in perfume and always had headaches and allergies and never seemed to think about the connection.

10

Once, a fellow detective had had an almost-fatal asthma attack after a clerical worker stood near him wearing what smelled like an entire bottle of perfume.

Gwendolyn stopped suddenly and he plowed into her, his hands sweeping out to grasp her shoulders and steady her before she fell from his momentum.

"Oh, sorry!" she exclaimed, and felt a thrill of pleasure at the warm strength of the big hands holding her so gently.

He removed them at once. "What is it?"

She had to force her mind to work. Detective Sergeant Marquez was very sexy and she'd been drawn to him since her first sight of him several weeks before. "I meant to ask if you wanted me to check with Alice Fowler over at the crime lab about the digital camera we found in the murdered woman's apartment. By now, she might have something on the trace evidence."

"Good idea. You do that."

"I'll swing past there on my way back to the office after lunch," she promised, and beamed, because it was a big case and he was letting her contribute to solving it. "Thanks."

He nodded, his mind already on the wonderful beef Stroganoff he was going to order at the nearby café where he usually had lunch. He'd been looking forward to it all week. It was Friday and he could splurge.

Tomorrow was his day off. He was going to spend it helping his mother, Barbara, process and can a bushel of hothouse tomatoes she'd been given by an organic gardener with a greenhouse. She owned Barbara's Café in Jacobsville, and she liked to use her organic vegetables and herbs in the meals she prepared for her clients. They would add to the store of canned summer tomatoes that she'd already processed earlier in the year.

He owed her a lot. He'd been orphaned in junior high school and Barbara Ferguson, who'd just lost her husband in an accident, and suffered a miscarriage, had taken him in. His mother had once worked for Barbara at the café just briefly. Then his parents—well, his mother and stepfather —had died in a wreck, leaving a single, lonely child all on his own. Rick had been a terrible teen, always in trouble, bad-tempered and moody. He'd been afraid when he lost his mother. He had no other living relatives of whom he was aware, and no place to go. Barbara had stepped in and given him a home. He loved her no less than he'd loved his real mother, and he was quite protective of her. He never spoke of his step-father. He tried not to remember him at all.

Barbara wanted him to marry and settle down and have a family. She harped on it all the time. She even introduced him to single women. Nothing helped. He seemed to be an eternally on-sale item in the matrimonial market that everybody bypassed for the fancier merchandise. He laughed shortly to himself at the thought.

Gwen watched him leave and wondered why he'd laughed. She was embarrassed that she'd thought he was asking her to lunch. He didn't seem to have a girlfriend and everybody joked about his nonexistent love life. But he wasn't attracted to Gwen in that way. It didn't matter. No man had ever liked her, really. She was everybody's confidante, the good girl who could give advice about how to please other women with small gifts and entertainments. But she was never asked out for herself.

She knew she wasn't pretty. She was always passed over for the flashy women, the assertive women, the powerful women. The women who didn't think sex before marriage was a sin. She'd had a man double over laughing when she'd told him that, after he expected a night in bed in return for a nice meal and the theater. Then he'd become angry, having spent so much money on her with nothing to show for it. The experience had soured her.

"Don Quixote," she murmured to herself. "I'm Don Quixote."

"Wrong sex," Detective Sergeant Gail Rogers said as she paused beside the newcomer. Rogers was the mother of some very wealthy ranchers in Comanche Wells, but she kept her job and her own income. She was an amazing peace officer.

Gwen admired her tremendously. "And what's that all about?" she asked.

Gwen sighed, glancing around to make sure they weren't being overheard. "I won't give out on dates," she whispered. "So men think I'm insane." She shrugged. "I'm Don Quixote, trying to restore morality and idealism to a decadent world."

Rogers didn't laugh. She smiled, very kindly. "He was noble, in his way. An idealist with a dream."

"He was nutty as a fruitcake." Gwen sighed.

"Yes, but he made everyone around him feel of worth, like the prostitute whom he idealized as a great lady for whom he quested," came the surprising reply. "He gave dreams to people who had given them up for harsh reality. He was adored by them."

Gwen laughed. "Yes, I suppose he wasn't so bad at that."

"People should have ideals, even if they get laughed at," Rogers added. "You stick to your guns. Every society has its outcasts." She leaned down. "Nobody who conformed to the rigid culture of any society ever made history."

Gwen brightened. "That's true." Then she added, "You've lived through a lot. You got shot," Gwen recalled hearing.

"I did. It was worthwhile, though. We broke a cold case wide-open and caught the murderer."

"I heard. That was some story."

Rogers smiled. "Indeed it was. Rick Marquez got blindsided and left for dead by the same scoundrels who shot me. But we both survived." She frowned. "What's wrong? Marquez giving you a hard time?"

"It's my own fault," Gwen confided. "I can't wear contacts and I hate glasses. I tripped in a crime scene and came close to contaminating some evidence." She grimaced. "It's a murder case, too, that college freshman they found dead in her apartment last night. The defense will have a field day with that when the perp is caught and brought to trial. And it will be my fault. I just got chewed out for it. I should have, too," she said quickly, because she didn't want Rogers to think Marquez was being unfair.

Rogers's dark eyes scarched hers. "You like your sergeant, don't you?"

"I respect him," Gwen said, and then flushcd helplessly.

Rogers studied her warmly. "He's a nice man," she said. "He does have a temper and he does take too many chances. But you'll get used to his moods."

"I'm working on that." Gwen chuckled.

"How did you like Atlanta?" Rogers asked conversationally as they headed for the exit.

"Excuse me?" Gwen said absently.

"Atlanta P.D. Where you were working."

"Oh. Oh!" Gwen had to think quickly. "It was

15

nice. I liked the department. But I wanted a change, and I've always wanted to see Texas."

"I see."

No, she didn't, Gwen thought, and thank goodness for that. Gwen was keeping secrets that she didn't dare divulge. She changed the subject as they walked together to the parking lot to their respective vehicles.

Lunch was a salad with dressing on the side, and half a grilled cheese sandwich. Dessert, and her drink, was a cappuccino. She loved the expensive coffee and could only afford it one day a week, on Fridays. She ate an inexpensive lunch so that she could have her coffee.

She sipped it with her eyes closed, smiling. It had an aroma that evoked Italy, a little sidewalk café in Rome with the ruins visible in the distance . . .

She opened her eyes at once and looked around, as if someone could see the thoughts in her head. She must be very careful not to mention that memory, or other similar ones, in regular conversation. She was a budding junior detective. She had to remember that. It wouldn't do to let anything slip at this crucial moment.

That thought led to thoughts of Detective Marquez and what would be a traumatic revelation for him when the time came for disclosure. Meanwhile, her orders were to observe him, keep her head down and try to discover how much he, or his adoptive mother, knew about his true background. She couldn't say anything. Not yet.

She finished her coffee, paid for her meal and walked out onto the chilly streets. So funny, she thought, the way the weather ran in cycles. It had been unseasonably cold throughout the South during the spring then came summer and blazing, unrelenting heat with drought and wildfires and cattle dying in droves. Now it was November and still unseasonably warm, but some weather experts said snow might come soon.

The weather was nuts. There had been epic drought throughout the whole southern tier of America, from Arizona to Florida, and there had been horrible wildfires in the southwestern states. Triple-digit temperatures had gone all summer in south Texas. There had been horrible flooding on the Mississippi River due to the large snowmelt, from last winter's unusually deep snows up north.

Now it was November and Gwen was actually sweating long before she reached her car, although it had been chilly this morning. She took off her jacket. At least the car had air-conditioning, and she was turning it on, even if it was technically almost winter. Idly, she wondered how people had lived in this heat before air-conditioning was invented. It couldn't have been an easy life, especially since most Texans of the early twentieth century had worked on the land.

Imagine, having to herd and brand cattle in this sort of heat, much less plow and plant!

Gwen got into her car and drove by the crime lab to see if Alice had found anything on that digital camera. In fact, she had. There were a lot of photos of people who were probably friends—Gwen could use face recognition software to identify them, hopefully—and there was one odd-looking man standing a little distance behind a couple who was smiling into the camera against the background of the apartment complex where the victim had lived. That was interesting and suspicious. She'd have to check that man out. He didn't look as if he belonged in such a setting. It was a mid-range apartment complex, and the man was dingy and ill kempt and staring a little too intently. She drove back to her precinct.

Her mind was still on Marquez, on what she knew, and he didn't. She hoped he wasn't going to have too hard a time with his true history, when the truth came out.

Barbara glared at her son. "Can't you just peel the tomato, sweetie, without taking out most of it except the core?"

He grimaced. "Sorry," he said, wielding the paring knife with more care as he went to work on what looked like a bushel of tomatoes, a gift from an organic gardener with a hothouse, that his mother was canning in her kitchen at home.

Canning jars simmered in a huge tub of water, getting ready to be filled with fragrant tomato slices and then processed in the big pressure cooker. He glared at it.

"I hate those things," he muttered. "Even the safest ones are dangerous."

"Baloney," she said inelegantly. "Give me those."

She took the bowl of tomatoes and dunked them into a pot of boiling water. She left them there for a couple of minutes and fished them out in a colander. She put them in the sink in front of Rick. "There. Now they'll skin. I keep telling you this is a more efficient way than trying to cut the skins off. But you don't listen, my dear."

"I like skinning them," he said with a dark-eyed smile in her direction. "It's an outlet for my frustrations."

"Oh?" She didn't look at him, deliberately. "What sort of frustrations?"

"There's this new woman at work," he said grimly.

"Gwen." She nodded.

He dropped the knife, picked it back up and stared at her.

"You talk about her all the time."

"I do?" It was news to him. He didn't realize that.

She nodded as she skinned tomatoes. "She trips over things that she doesn't see, she messes up crime scenes, she spills coffee, she can't find her cell phone . . ." She glanced at him. He was still standing there, with the knife poised over a tomato. "Get busy, there, those tomatoes won't peel themselves."

He groaned.

"Just think how nice they'll taste in one of my beef stew recipes," she coaxed. "Go on, peel."

"Why can't we just get one of those things that sucks the air out of bags and freeze them instead?"

"What if we have a major power outage that lasts for days and days?" she returned.

He thought for a minute. "I'll go buy twenty bags of ice and several of those foam coolers."

She laughed. "Yes, but we can't tell how the power grid is going to cope if we have one of those massive CMEs like the Carrington Event in 1859."

He blinked. "Excuse me?"

"There was a massive coronal mass ejection in 1859 called the Carrington Event," she explained. "When it hit earth, all the electrics on the planet went crazy. Telegraph lines burned up and telegraph units caught fire." She glanced at him. "There wasn't much electricity back in those days—it was in its infancy. But imagine if such a thing happened today, with our dependence on electricity. Everything is connected to the grid these days, banks, communications corporations, pharmacies, government, military and the list goes on and on. Even our water and power are

20

controlled by computers. Just imagine if we had no way to access our computers."

He whistled. "I was in the grocery store one day when the computers went offline. They couldn't process credit cards. Most people had to leave. I had enough cash for bread and milk. Then another time the computers in the pharmacy went down, when you had to have those antibiotics for the sinus infection last winter. I had to come home and get the checkbook and go back. People without credit cards had real problems."

"See?" She went back to her tomatoes.

"I suppose it would be a pretty bad thing. Is it going to happen, you think?"

"Someday, certainly. The sun has eleven year cycles, you know, with a solar minimum and a solar maximum. The next solar maximum, some scientists say, is in 2012. If we're going to get hit, that would have my vote for the timeline."

"Twenty-twelve," he groaned, rolling his eyes. "We had this guy come in the office and tell us we needed to put out a flyer."

"What about?"

"The fact that the world is ending in 2012 and we have to have tin-foil hats to protect us from electromagnetic pulses."

"Ah. EMPs," she said knowledgeably. "Actually, I think you'd have to be in a modified and greatly enlarged version of a Leiden jar to be fully protected. So would any computer equipment you wanted to save." She glanced at him. "They're developing weapons like that, you know," she added. "All it would take is one nicely placed EMP and our military computers would go down like tenpins."

He put down the knife. "Where do you learn all this stuff?" he asked, exasperated.

"On the internet." She pulled an iPod out of her pocket and showed it to him. "I have Wi-Fi in the house, you know. I just connect to all the appropriate websites." She checked her book-marks. "I have one for space weather, three radars for terrestrial weather and about ten covert sites that tell you all the stuff the government won't tell you . . ."

"My mother, the conspiracy theorist," he moaned.

"You won't hear this stuff on the national news," she said smartly. "The mainstream media is controlled by three major corporations. They decide what you'll get to hear. And mostly it's what entertainer got drunk, what television show is getting the ratings and what politician is patting himself on the back or running for reelection. In my day—" she warmed to her theme "—we had real news on television. It was local and we had real reporters out gathering it. Like the Jacobsville paper still does," she added.

"I know about the Jacobsville paper," he said with a sigh. "We hear that Cash Grier spends most of his time trying to protect the owner from getting assassinated. She knows all the drug distribution points and the drug lords by name, and she's printing them." He shook his head. "She's going to be another statistic one day. They've killed plenty of newspaper publishers and reporters over the border for less. She's rocking the boat."

"Somebody needs to rock it," Barbara muttered as she peeled another tomato skin off and tossed it into a green bag to be used for mulch in her garden. She never wasted any organic refuse. "People are dying so that another generation can become addicted to drugs."

"I can't argue that point," he said. "The problem is that nothing law enforcement is doing is making much of a dent in drug trafficking. If there's a market, there's going to be a supply. That's just the way things are."

"They say Hayes Carson actually talked to Minette Raynor about it."

That was real news. Minette owned the *Jacobsville Times*. She had two stepsiblings, Shane, who was twelve, and Julie, who was six. She'd loved her stepmother very much. Her stepmother and her father had died within weeks of each other, leaving a grieving Minette with two little children to raise, a newspaper to run and a ranch to manage. She had a manager to handle the ranch, and her great-aunt Sarah lived with her and took care of the kids after school so that Minette could keep working. Minette was twenty-five now and unmarried. She and Hayes Carson didn't get along. Hayes blamed her, God knew why, for his younger brother's drug-related death, even after Rachel Conley left a confession stating that she'd given Bobby Carson, Hayes's brother, the drugs that killed him.

Rick chuckled. "If there's ever a border war, Minette will stand in the street pointing a finger at Hayes so the invaders can get him first."

"I wonder," Barbara mused. "Sometimes I think where there's antagonism, there's also something deeper. I've seen people who hate each other end up married."

"Cash Grier and his Tippy," Rick mused.

"Yes, and Stuart York and Ivy Conley."

"Not to mention half a dozen others. Jacobsville is growing by leaps and bounds."

"So is Comanche Wells. We've got new people there, too." She was peeling faster. "Did you notice that Grange bought a ranch in Comanche Wells, next to the property that his boss owns?"

Rick pursed his sensual lips. "Which boss?"

She blinked at him. "What do you mean, which boss?"

"He works as ranch manager for Jason Pendleton. But he also works on the side for Eb Scott," he said. "You didn't hear this from me, but he was involved in the Pendleton kidnapping," he added. "He went to get Gracie Pendleton back when she was kidnapped by that exiled South American dictator, Emilio Machado."

"Machado."

"Yes." He peeled the tomato slowly. "He's a conundrum."

"What do you mean?"

"He started out, we learned, as a farm laborer down in Mexico, from the time he was about ten years old. He was involved in protests against foreign interests even as a teenager. But he got tired of scratching dirt for a living. He could play the guitar and sing, so he worked bars for a while and then through a contact, he got a job as an entertainer on a cruise ship. That got boring. He signed on with a bunch of mercs and became known internationally as a crusader against oppression. Afterward, he went to South America and hired on with another paramilitary group that was fighting to preserve the way of life of the native people in Barrera, a little nation in the Amazon bordering Peru. He helped the paramilitary unit free a tribe of natives from a foreign corporation that was trying to kill them to get the oil-rich land on which they were living. He developed a taste for defending the underdog, moved up in the ranks of the military until he became a general." He smiled. "It seems that he was a natural leader, because when the small country's president died four years ago, Machado was elected by acclamation." He glanced at her. "Do you realize how rare that is, even for a small nation?"

"If people loved him so much, how is it that he's in Mexico kidnapping people to get money to retake his country?"

"He wasn't ousted by the people, but by a vicious and bloodthirsty military subordinate who knew when and how to strike, while Machado was on a trip to a neighboring country to sign a trade agreement and offer an alliance against foreign corporate takeovers."

"I didn't know that."

"It's sort of privileged info, so you can't share it," he told her. "Anyway, the subordinate killed Machado's entire staff, and sent his secret police to shut down newspapers and television and radio stations. Overnight, influential people ended up in prison. Educators, politicians, writers—anyone who might threaten the new regime. There have been hundreds of murders, and now the subordinate, Pedro Mendez by name, is allying himself with drug lords in a neighboring country. It seems that cocaine grows quite nicely in Barrera and poor farmers are being 'encouraged' to grow it instead of food crops on their land. Mendez is also nationalizing every single business so that he has absolute control."

"No wonder the general is trying to retake his country," she said curtly. "I hope he makes it."

"So do I," Rick replied. "But I can't say that in

public," he added. "He's wanted in this country for kidnapping. It's a capital offense. If he's caught and convicted he could wind up with a death penalty."

She winced. "I don't condone how he's getting the money," she replied. "But he's going to use it for a noble reason."

"Noble." He chuckled.

"That's not funny," she said shortly.

"I'm not laughing at the word. It's Gwen. She goes around mumbling that she's Don Quixote."

She laughed out loud. "What?"

He shook his head. "Rogers told me. It seems that our newest detective won't give out on dates and she groups herself with Don Quixote, who tried to restore honor and morality to a decadent world."

"My, my!" She pursed her lips and smiled secretively.

"I don't want to marry Gwen Cassaway," he said at once. "I just thought I'd mention that, because I can read minds, and I don't like what you're thinking."

"She's a nice girl."

"She's a woman."

"She's a nice girl. She has a very idealistic and romantic attitude for someone who lives in the city. And I ought to know. I have women from cities coming through here all the time, talking about unspeakable things right in public with the whole world listening." Her lips made a thin line. "Do you know, Grange was having lunch next to a table of them where they were discussing men's, well, intimate men parts," she amended, clearing her throat, "and Grange got up from his chair, told them what he thought of them for discussing a bedroom topic in public in front of decent people and he walked out."

"What did they do?"

"One of them laughed. One of the others cried. Another said he needed to start living in the real world instead of small town 'stupidville.'" She grinned. "Of course, she said it after he'd already left. While he was talking, they didn't say a word. But they left soon after. I was glad. I can't choose my clientele and I've only ever ordered one person to leave my restaurant since I've owned it," she added.

She dragged herself back to the present. "But the topic of conversation was getting to me, too. People need to talk about intimate things in private, not in a public place with their voices raised. We don't all think alike."

"Only in some ways," he pointed out, and hugged her impulsively. "You're a nice mother. I'm so lucky to have you for an adoptive parent."

She hugged him back. "You've enriched my life, my sweet." She sighed, closing her eyes in his warm embrace. "When I lost Bart, I wanted to die, too. And then your mother and stepfather died, and there you were, as alone as I was. We needed each other."

"We did." He moved away and smiled affectionately. "You took on a big burden with me. I was a bad boy."

She groaned and rolled her eyes. "Were you ever! Always in fights, in school and out. I spent half my life in the principal's office and once at a school board meeting where they were going to vote to throw you right out of school altogether and put you in alternative school." Her face hardened. "In their dreams!"

"Yes, you took a lawyer to the meeting and buffaloed them. First time it ever happened, I heard later."

"I was very mad."

"I felt really bad about that," he said. "But I put my nose to the grindstone after, and tried hard to make it up to you."

"Joined the police force, went to night school and got your associate degree, went to the San Antonio Police Department and worked your way up in the ranks to sergeant," she agreed, smiling. "Made me *so* proud!"

He hugged her again. "I owe it all to you."

"No. You owe it to your hard work. I may have helped, but you pulled yourself up."

He kissed her forehead. "Thank you. For everything."

"You're my son. I love you very much."

He cleared his throat. Emotions were difficult for him, especially considering his job. "Yeah. Me, too."

She grinned. The smile faded as she searched his large, dark eyes. "Do you ever wonder about your mother's past?"

His eyebrows shot up. "What a question!" He frowned. "What do you mean?"

"Do you know anything about her friends? About any male friends she had before she married your stepfather?"

He shrugged. "Not really. She didn't talk about her relationships. Well, I wasn't old enough for her to confide in me, either, you know. She never was one to talk about intimate things," he said quietly. "Not even about my real father. She said that he died, but she never talked about him. She was very young when I was born. She did say she'd done things she wanted forgiveness for, and she went to confession a lot." He studied her closely. "You must have had some reason for asking me that."

She put her lips tightly together. "Something I overheard. I wasn't supposed to be listening."

"Come on, tell me," he said when she hesitated.

"Cash Grier was having lunch with some fed. They were discussing Machado. The fed mentioned a woman named Dolores Ortíz who had some connection to General Machado when he lived in Mexico."

CHAPTER 2

"Dolores Ortíz?" he asked, the paring knife poised in midair. "That was my mother's maiden name."

"I know."

Rick frowned. "You mean my mother might have been romantically involved with Emilio Machado?"

"I got that impression," Barbara said, nodding. "But I wasn't close enough to hear the entire conversation. I just got bits and pieces of it."

He pursed his lips. "Well, my father died around the time I was born, so it's not impossible that she did meet Machado in Mexico. Although, it's a big country."

"You lived in the state of Sonora," she pointed out. "That's where Machado had his truck farm, they said."

He finished skinning the tomato and reached for another one. "Wouldn't that be a coincidence, if my mother actually knew him?"

"Yes, it would."

"Well, it was a long time ago," he said easily. "And she's dead, and I never knew him. So what good would it do for them to dig up an old romance now?"

"I have no idea. It bothered me, a little. I mean, you're my son."

"Yes, I am." He glanced at her. "I love it when people get all flustered and start babbling when you introduce me. You're blonde and fair and I'm dark and obviously Hispanic."

"You're gorgeous, my baby," she teased. "I just wish women would stop crying on your shoulder about other men and start trying to marry you."

He sighed. "Chance would be a fine thing. I carry a gun!" he said with mock horror.

She glowered at him. "All off-duty policemen carry guns."

"Yes, but I might shoot somebody accidentally, and it would get in the way if I tried to hug somebody."

"I gather that somebody female mentioned that?"

He sighed and nodded. "A public defender," he said. "She thought I was cute, but she doesn't date men who carry. It's a principle, she said. She hates guns."

"I hate guns, too, but I keep a shotgun in the closet in case I ever need to defend myself," Barbara pointed out.

"I'll defend you."

"You work in San Antonio," she said. "If you're not here, I have to defend myself. By the time Hayes Carson could get to my place, I'd be . . .

well, not in any good condition if somebody tried to harm me."

That had happened once, Rick recalled with anger. A man he'd arrested, after he'd been released, had gone after Rick's adoptive mother for revenge. It was just chance that Hayes Carson had stopped by when he was off duty, in his unmarked truck, to ask her about catering an event. The ex-convict had piled out of his car and come right up on the porch with a drawn gun—in violation of parole—and banged on the door demanding that Barbara come outside. Hayes had come outside, disarmed him, cuffed him and taken him right to jail. The man was now serving another term in prison, for assault on a police officer, trespassing, attempted assault, possessing a firearm in violation of parole and resisting arrest. Barbara had testified at his trial. So had Hayes.

Rick shook his head. "I hate having you in danger because of my job."

"It was only the one time," she said, comforting him. "It could have been somebody who carried a grudge because their apple pie wasn't served with ice cream or something."

He smiled. "Dream on. You even make the ice cream you serve with it. Your pies are out of this world."

"Don't you have an in-house seminar coming up at work?" she asked.

He nodded.

"Why don't you take a couple of pies back with you?"

"That would be nice. Thank you."

"My pleasure." She pursed her lips. "Does Gwen like apple pie?"

He turned and stared at her. "Gwen is a colleague. I never, never date colleagues."

She sighed. "Okay."

He went back to work on the tomatoes. This could turn into a problem. His mother, well-meaning and loving, nevertheless was determined to get him married. That was one area in which he wanted to do his own prospecting. And never in this lifetime did he want to end up with someone like Gwen, who had two left feet and the dress sense of a Neanderthal woman. He laughed at the idea of her in bearskins carrying a spear. But he didn't share the joke with his mother.

When he went to work the next day, it was qualifying time on the firing range. Rick was a good shot, and he kept excellent care of his service weapon. But the testing was one of the things he really hated about police work.

His lieutenant, Cal Hollister, could outshoot any man in the precinct. He scored a hundred percent regularly. Rick could usually manage in the nineties but never a perfect score. He always seemed to do the qualifying when the lieutenant was doing his, and his ego suffered.

Today, Gwen Cassaway also showed up. Rick tried not to groan out loud. Gwen would drop her pistol, accidentally kill the lieutenant and Rick would be prosecuted for manslaughter . . .

"Why are you groaning like that?" Hollister asked curtly as he checked the clip for his .45 in preparation for target shooting.

"Just a stray thought, sir, nothing important." His eyes went involuntarily to Gwen, who was also loading her own pistol.

On the firing range, shooters wore eye protection and ear protection. They customarily loaded only six bullets into the clip of the automatic, and this was done at the time they got into position to fire. The pistol would be held at low or medium ready position, after being carefully drawn from its snapped holster for firing, with the safety on. The pistol, even unloaded, would never be pointed in any direction except that of the target and the trigger finger would never rest on the trigger. When in firing position, the safety would be released, and the shooter would fire at the target using either the Weaver, modified Weaver, or Isosceles shooting stance.

One of the most difficult parts of shooting, and one of the most important to master, was trigger pull. The pressure exerted on the trigger had to be perfect in order to place a shot correctly. There were graphs on the firing range that helped participants check the efficiency of their trigger pull and help to improve it. Rick's was improving. But his lieutenant consistently showed him up on the gun range, and it made him uncomfortable. He tried not to practice or qualify when the other man was around. Unfortunately, he always seemed to be on the range when Rick was.

Hollister followed Rick's gaze to Gwen. He knew, as Rick did, that she had some difficulty with coordination. He pursed his lips. His black eyes danced as he glanced covertly at Gwen. "It's okay, Marquez. We're insured," he said under his breath.

Rick cleared his throat and tried not to laugh.

Hollister moved onto the firing line. His thick blond hair gleamed like pale honey in the sunlight. He glanced at Gwen. "Ready, Detective?" he drawled, pulling the heavy ear protectors on over his hair.

Gwen gave him a nice smile. "Ready when you are, sir."

The Range Master moved into position, indicated that everything was ready and gave the signal to fire.

Hollister, confident and relaxed, chuckled, aimed at the target and proceeded to blow the living hell out of it.

Rick, watching Gwen worriedly, saw something incredible happen next. Gwen snapped into a modified Weaver position, barely even aimed and threw six shots into the center of the target with pinpoint accuracy.

His mouth flew open.

She took the clip out of her automatic, checked the cylinder and waited for the Range Master to check her score.

"Cassaway," he said eventually, and hesitated. "One hundred percent."

Rick and the lieutenant stared at each other.

"Lieutenant Hollister," the officer continued, and was obviously trying not to smile, "ninety-nine percent."

"What the hell . . . !" Hollister burst out. "I hit dead center!"

"Missed one, sir, by a hair," the officer replied with a twinkle in his eyes. "Sorry."

Hollister let out a furious bad word. Gwen marched right up to him and glared at him from pale green eyes.

"Sir, I find that word offensive and I'd appreciate it if you would refrain from using it in my presence," she said curtly.

Hollister's high cheekbones actually flushed. Rick tensed, waiting for the explosion.

But Hollister didn't erupt. His black eyes smiled down at the rookie detective. "Point taken, Detective," he said, and his deep voice was even pleasant. "I apologize."

Gwen swallowed. She was almost shaking. "Thank you, sir."

She turned and walked off.

"Not bad shooting, by the way," he commented as he removed the clip from his own pistol.

She grinned. "Thanks." She glanced at Rick, who was still gaping, and almost made a smart remark. But she thought better of it in time.

Rick let out the breath he'd been holding. "She trips over her own feet," he remarked. "But that was some damned fine shooting."

"It was," the lieutenant agreed. He shook his head. "You can never figure people, can you, Marquez?"

"True, sir. Very true."

Later that day, Rick noted two dignified men in suits walking past his office. They glanced at him, spoke to one another and hesitated. One gestured down the hall quickly, and they kept walking.

He wondered what in the world was going on.

Rogers came into his office a few minutes later, frowning. "Odd thing."

"What?" he asked, his eyes on his computer screen where he was running a case through VICAP.

"Did you see those two suits?"

"Yes, they hesitated outside my office. Who are they, feds?"

"Yes. State Department."

He burst out laughing as he looked at her with

large, dancing brown eyes. "They think I'm illegal and they're here to bust me?"

"Stop that," she muttered.

"Sorry. Couldn't resist it." He turned to her. "We have high level immigration cases all the time where the State Department gets involved."

"Yes, but mostly we deal with the enforcement branch of the Department of Immigration and Naturalization, with ICE. Or we deal with the DEA in drug cases, I know that. But these guys aren't from Austin. They're from D.C."

"The capitol?"

"That's right. They've been talking to the lieutenant all morning. They're taking him to lunch, too."

"What's going on? Any idea?"

She shook her head. "Only that gossip says they're on the Machado case."

"Yes. He's wanted for kidnapping." He didn't add what Barbara had told him, that his own birth mother might have once known Machado in the past.

"He's not in the country."

"And how would you know that?" Rick asked her with pursed lips. "Another psychic insight?" he added, because she had a really unusual sixth sense about cases.

"No. I ran into Cash Grier over at the courthouse. He was up here on a case."

"Our police chief from Jacobsville," he acknowledged.

"The very same. He mentioned that Jason Pendleton's foreman is on temporary leave because of Machado."

"Grange," Rick recalled, naming the foreman. "He went into Mexico to retrieve Gracie Pendleton when she was kidnapped by Machado's men for ransom."

"Yes. It seems the general took a liking to him, had him investigated and offered him a job."

Rick blinked. "Excuse me?"

"That's what I said when Grier told me." She laughed. "The general really does have style. He said somebody had to organize his mercs when he goes in to retake his country. Grange, being a former major in the army, seemed the logical choice."

"His country is Barrera," Rick mused. "Nice name, since it sits on the Amazon River bordering Colombia, Peru and Bolivia. Barrera is Spanish for barrier."

"I didn't know that, only having completed two years of college Spanish," she replied blithely.

He made a face at her.

"Anyway, it seems Grange likes the idea of being a crusader for democracy and freedom and human rights, so he took the job. He's in Mexico at the moment helping the general come up with a plan of attack."

"With Eb Scott offering candidates, I don't doubt," Rick added. "He's got the cream of the crop at his counterterrorism training center in Jacobsville, as far as mercs go."

"The general is gathering them from everywhere. He has a couple of former SAS from Great Britain, a one-eyed terror from South Africa named Rourke whose nickname is Deadeye . . ."

"I know him," Rick said.

"Me, too," Rogers replied. "He's a pill, isn't he? Rumored to be the natural son of K. C. Kantor, who was one of the more successful ex-mercs."

"Yes, Kantor became a billionaire after he gave up the lifestyle. He has a daughter who married Dr. Micah Steele in Jacobsville, and a godchild who married into the ranching Callister family up in Montana." His eyes narrowed. "Where is the general getting the money to finance his revolution?"

"Remember that he gave Gracie back without any payment. But then he nabbed Jason Pendleton for ransom, and Gracie paid it with the money from her trust fund?"

"Forgot about that," Rick said.

"It ran to six figures. So he's bankrolled. We hear he also charged what's left of the Fuentes cartel for protection while he was sharing space with them over the border."

"Charging drug lords rent in their own turf?" Rick asked.

"And getting it. The general has a pretty fearsome reputation," she added. She laughed.

"He's also a incredibly handsome," she mused. "I've seen a photograph of him. They say he has a charming personality, reveres women and plays the guitar and sings like an angel."

"A man of many talents."

"Not the least of which is inspiring troops." Rogers sighed. "But it has to be unsettling for the State Department, especially since the Mexican government is up in arms about having Machado recruit mercs to invade a sovereign nation in South America while living in their country."

"Why are they protesting to us? We aren't helping him," Rick pointed out.

"He's on our border."

"If they want us to do something about Machado, they could do something about the militant drug cartels running over our borders with automatic weapons to protect their drug runners."

"Chance would be a fine thing."

"I guess so. None of that explains why the State Department is gumming up our office," he added. "This is San Antonio. The border is that way." He pointed out the window. "A long, long drive that way."

"I know. That's what puzzled me. So I pumped Grier for information."

"What did he tell you?"

"He didn't. Tell me anything," she added grimly. "So I had my oldest son pump his best friend, Sheriff Hayes Carson, for information."

"Did you get anything from him?"

She bit her lower lip. "Bits and pieces." She gave him a worried look. She couldn't tell him what she found out. She'd been sworn to secrecy. "But nothing really concrete, I'm sorry to say."

"I suppose they'll tell us eventually."

"I suppose so."

"When is this huge invasion of Barrera going to take place? Any timeline on that?"

"None that presented itself." She sighed. "But it's going to be a gala occasion, from what we hear. The State Department would have good reason to be concerned. They can't back a revolution . . ."

"One of the letter agencies could help with that, of course, without public acknowledgment."

Letter agencies referred to government bureaus like the CIA, which Rick assumed would have been in the forefront of any assistance they could legally give to help install a democratic government friendly to the United States in South America.

"Kilraven used to belong to the CIA," Rick murmured. "Maybe I could ask him if he knows anything."

"I'd keep my nose out of it for the time being," Rogers cautioned, foreseeing trouble ahead if Rick tried to interfere at this stage of the game. "We'll know soon enough."

"I guess so." He glanced at her and asked, "Hear

about what happened on the firing range this morning?"

Her eyes brightened. "Did I ever! The whole department's talking about it. Our rookie detective outshot the lieutenant."

"By a whole point." Rick grinned. "Imagine that. She falls into potted plants and trips over crime evidence, but she can shoot like an Old West gunslinger." He shook his head. "I thought I'd pass out when she started firing that automatic. It was beautiful. She never even seemed to aim. Just snapped off the shots and hit in the center every single time."

"The lieutenant's a good loser, though," Rogers commented. "He bought a single pink rose and laid it on her desk after lunch."

Rick's eyes narrowed and his expression grew cold. "Did he, now?"

The lieutenant was a widower. Nobody knew how he lost his wife, he never spoke of her. He didn't even date, as far as anyone knew. And here he was giving flowers to Gwen, who was young and innocent and impressionable . . .

"I said, do you think that could be construed as sexual harassment?" Rogers repeated.

"He gave her a flower!"

"Well, yes, but he wouldn't have given a man a flower, would he?"

"I'd have given Kilraven a flower after he nabbed the perp who blindsided me in the alley

44

and left me for dead," he said, tongue in cheek.

She sighed. She felt in her pocket for the unopened pack of cigarettes she kept there, pulled it out and looked at it with sad eyes. "I miss smoking. The kids made me quit."

"You're still carrying around cigarettes?" he exclaimed.

"Well, it's comforting. Having them in my pocket, I mean. I wouldn't actually smoke one, of course. Unless we have a nuclear attack, or something. Then it would be okay."

He burst out laughing. "You're incorrigible, Rogers."

"Only on Mondays," she said after a minute. She glanced at her watch. "I have to get back to work."

"Let me know if you find out anything else, okay?"

"Of course I will." She smiled.

She felt a twinge of guilt as she walked out of his office. She wished she could tell him the truth, or at least prepare him for what she knew was coming. He had a surprise in store. Probably not a very nice one.

"But I made corned beef and cabbage," Barbara groaned when Rick phoned her Friday afternoon to say he wasn't coming home that night.

"I know, it's my favorite, and I'm sorry," he said. "But we've got a stakeout. I have to go. It's my squad." He sighed. "Gwen's on it, and she'll probably knock over a trash can and we'll get burned."

"You have to think positively." She hesitated. "You could bring her home with you tomorrow. The corned beef will still be good and I'll cook more cabbage."

"She's a colleague," he repeated. "I don't date colleagues."

"Does your lieutenant date colleagues?" she asked with glee. "Because I heard he left her a single rose on her desk. What a lovely, romantic man!"

He gnashed his teeth and hoped the sound didn't carry. He was tired of hearing that story. It had gone the rounds at work all week.

"You could put a rose on her desk . . ."

"If I did, it would be attached to a pink slip!" he snapped.

She gasped, hesitated and turned off the phone. It was the first time he'd ever snapped at her.

Rick groaned and dialed her number back. It rang and rang. "Come on. Please?" he spoke into the busy signal. "I'm sorry. Come on, let me apologize . . ."

"Yes?" Barbara answered stiffly.

"I'm sorry. I didn't mean to snap at you. I really didn't. I'll come home for lunch tomorrow and eat corned beef and cabbage. I'll even eat crow.

Raw." There was silence on the end of the line. "I'll bring a rose?"

She laughed. "Okay, you're forgiven."

"I'm really sorry. Things have been hectic at work. But that's no excuse for being rude to you."

"No, it's not. But I'm not mad."

"You're a nice mother."

She laughed. "You're a nice son. I love you. I'll see you at lunch tomorrow."

"Have a good night."

"You have a careful one," she said solemnly. "Even rude sons are hard to come by these days," she added.

"I'll change my ways. Honest. See you."

"See you."

He hung up and sighed heavily. He couldn't imagine why he'd been so short with his own mother. Perhaps he needed a vacation. He only took time off when he was threatened. He loved his job. Being sergeant of an eight-detective squad in the Homicide Unit, in the Murder/Attempted Murder detail, was heady and satisfying. He assigned lead detectives to cases, reviewed cases to make sure everything necessary was done and kept up with what seemed like tons of paperwork, as well as reporting to the lieutenant on case-loads. But maybe a little time off would improve his temper. He'd talk to the lieutenant about it next week, he resolved. For now, he had work to do.

• • •

Gwen had been assigned as lead detective on the college student's murder case downtown. It was an odd sort of case. The woman had been stabbed by person or persons unknown, in her own apartment, with all the doors locked and the windows shut. There were no signs of a struggle. She was a pretty young woman with no current boyfriend, no apparent enemies, who led a quiet life and didn't party.

Gwen wanted very much to solve the case. She'd told Rick that Alice Fowler had found prints on a digital camera that featured an out-of-place man in the background. Gwen was checking that out. She was really working hard on the mystery.

But in the meantime, she'd been pressed into service to help Rick with a stakeout of a man wanted for shooting a police officer in a traffic stop. The officer lived, but he'd be in rehab for months. They had intel that the shooter was hiding out in a low class apartment building downtown with some help from an associate. But they couldn't find him there. So Rick decided to stake out the place and try to catch him. The fact that it was a Friday night meant that the younger, single detectives were trying to find ways not to get involved. Even the night detectives had excuses, pending cases that they simply couldn't spare time away from. So Rick ended up with Gwen and one young and eager patrol officer, Ted Sims, from the Patrol South Division who'd volunteered, hoping to find favor with Rick and maybe get a chance at climbing the ladder, and working as a detective one day.

They were set up in a ratty apartment downtown, observing a suspect across the alley in another run-down apartment building. They had all the lights off, a telescope, a video camera, listening devices, warrants to allow the listening devices, and as much black coffee as three detectives could drink in an evening. Which was quite a lot.

"I wish we had a pizza." Officer Sims sighed.

Rick sighed, too. "So do I, but the smell would carry and the perp would know we were watching him."

"Maybe we could put the pizza outside his door and he'd go nuts smelling it and rush out to grab it and we could grab him," Sims mused.

"What do you have in that bottle besides water?" Gwen asked, with twinkling green eyes.

Sims made a face. "Just water, sadly. I could really use a cold beer."

"Shut up," Marquez groaned. "I'm dying for one."

"We could ask Detective Cassaway to investigate the beer rack at the local convenience store and confiscate a six-pack for the crime scene investigation unit," Sims joked. "Nobody would have to know. We could threaten the owner with health violations or something."

Gwen gave him a cold look. "We don't steal."

Marquez gave him an even more vicious look. "Ever."

He flushed. "Hey," he said, holding up both hands, "I was just kidding!"

"I'm not laughing," she returned, unblinking.

"Neither am I," Marquez seconded. His face was hard with suppressed anger. "I don't want to hear talk like that from a sworn police officer."

"Sorry," he said, swallowing hard. "Really. Bad joke. I didn't mean I'd actually do it."

Gwen shrugged. Sims was very young. "I'm missing that new science fiction show I got hooked on," she groaned. "It's making me twitchy."

"I watch that one, too," Rick replied. "It's not bad."

"You could record it," Sims suggested. "Don't you have a DVR?"

She shook her head. "I'm poor. I can't afford one."

Rick glared at her. "We work for one of the best-paying departments in the southwest," he rattled off. "We have a benefits package, expense accounts, access to excellent vehicles . . ."

"I have a monthly rent bill, a monthly insurance bill, a car payment, utilities payments and I have to buy bullets for my gun," she muttered. "Who can afford luxuries?" She glared at him. "I haven't had a new suit in six months. This one looks like moths have nested in it already."

Rick's eyebrows arched up. "Surely, you've got more than one suit, Cassaway."

"Two suits, twelve blouses, six pair of shoes and assorted . . . other things," she said. "Mix and match and I'm sick of all of it. I want haute couture!"

"Good luck with that," Rick remarked.

"Luck won't do it."

"Hey, is this the guy we're looking for?" Sims asked suddenly, looking through the telescope.

CHAPTER 3

Rick and Gwen joined him at the window. Rick snapped a photo of the man across the street, using the telephoto feature, plugged it into his small computer and, using a new face recognition software component, compared it to the man he'd photographed.

"Positive ID. That's him," Rick said. "Let's go get him."

They ran down the steps, deploying quickly to the designations planned earlier by Rick.

The man, yawning and oblivious, stepped out onto the sidewalk next to a bus stop sign.

"Now," Rick yelled.

Three people came running toward the stunned man, who started to run, but it was far too late. Rick tackled him and took him down. He cuffed his hands behind his back and chuckled as the man started cursing.

"I ain't done nothin'!" he wailed.

"Then you don't have a thing to worry about."

The man only groaned.

"That was a nice takedown," Gwen said as they cleared their equipment out of the rented apartment, after the man had been taken away by the patrol officer.

"Thanks. I try to keep in shape."

She didn't dare look at him. She was having a hard enough time not noticing how very attractive he was.

"You know," he mused, "that was some fine shooting down at HQ."

She beamed. "Thanks." She glanced up. "At least I do have one saving grace."

"Probably more than one, Cassaway."

She shouldered her purse. "Are we done for the night?"

"Yes. I'll input the report and you can sign it tomorrow. I snapped at my mother. I have to go home and try to make it up to her."

"She's very nice."

He turned, frowning. "How do you know?"

"I came through Jacobsville when I had to interview a witness in that last murder trial," she reminded him. "I had lunch at the café. It's the only one in town, except for the Chinese restaurant, and I like her apple pie." She added that last bit to make sure he knew she wasn't frequenting his mother's café just because she was his mother.

"Oh."

"Has she owned the restaurant a long time?"

He nodded. "She opened it a couple of years before I was orphaned. My mother worked for her as a cook just briefly."

Gwen nodded, trying to be low-key. "Is your mother still alive? Your biological mother?" she asked while looking through her purse for her car keys.

"She and my stepfather died in a wreck when I was almost in my teens. Barbara had just lost her husband and had a miscarriage the month before it happened. She was grieving and so was I. Since I had no other family, and she knew me, she adopted me."

She flushed. "Oh. Sorry, I didn't mean to pry. I was just curious."

He shrugged. "Most everybody knows," he said easily. "I was born in Mexico, in Sonora, but my mother and stepfather came to this country when I was a toddler and lived in Jacobsville. My stepfather worked at one of the local ranches."

"What did he do?"

"Broke horses." The way he said it was cold and short, as if he didn't like being reminded of the man.

"I had an uncle who worked ranches in Wyoming," she confided. "He's dead now."

He studied her through narrowed eyes. "Wyoming. But you're from Atlanta?"

"Not originally."

He waited.

She cleared her throat. "My people are from Montana, originally."

"You're a long way from home."

"Yes, well, my parents moved to Maryland when I was small."

"I guess you miss the ocean."

She nodded. "A lot. It wasn't a long drive from our house. But I go where they send me. I've worked a lot of places—" She stopped dead, and could have bitten her tongue.

His eyebrows were arching already. "The Atlanta P.D. moves you around the country?"

"I mean, I've worked a lot of places around Atlanta."

"Mmm-hmm."

"I didn't always work for Atlanta P.D.," she muttered, trying to backpedal. "I worked for a risk organization for a year or two, in the insurance business, and they sent me around the country on jobs."

"A risk organization? What sort of work did you do?"

"I was a sort of security consultant." It wasn't quite the truth, but it wasn't quite a lie, either. She glanced at her watch as a diversion. "Oh, goodness, I'll miss my television show!"

"God forbid," he said dryly. "Okay. We're done here."

"It didn't take as long as I expected," she

commented on the way out. "Usually stakeouts last for hours if not days."

"Tell me about it," he said drolly. "Is your car close by?"

She turned at the foot of the steps. "It's across the street, thanks," she said, because she knew he was offering to walk her to it. He was a gentleman, in the nicest sort of way.

He nodded. "I'll see you Monday, then."

She smiled. "Yes, sir."

She turned and walked away. Her heart was pounding and she was cursing herself mentally. She'd almost blown the whole thing sky-high!

Barbara was her usual, smiling self, but her eyes were sad when Rick showed up at the door the night before he was due home.

"You said tomorrow?" she murmured.

He stepped into the house and hugged her, hard, rocking her in his arms. He heard a muffled sob. "I felt bad," he said at her ear. "I upset you."

"Hey," she murmured, drawing away to dab at her eyes, "that's what kids are supposed to do."

He smiled. "No, it's not."

"Want some coffee?"

"Yes!" he said at once, pulling off his suit coat and loosening his tie as he followed her to the kitchen. He swung the coat around one of the high-back kitchen chairs at the table and sat down. "I've been on stakeout, with convenience-store coffee." He made a face. "I think they keep it in the pot all day to make sure it doesn't pass for hot brown water."

She laughed as she made a fresh pot. "There's that profit margin to consider," she mused.

"I guess."

"Did you catch a crook?"

"We did, actually. That new face recognition software we use is awesome. Pegged the guy almost immediately."

"New technology." She shook her head. "Cameras everywhere, face recognition software, pat downs at the airport . . ." She turned and looked at him. "Isn't all that supposed to make us feel safer?"

"No, it's supposed to actually make you safer," he corrected. "It makes it harder for the bad guys to hide from the law."

"I guess so." She got out cups and saucers. "I made apple pie."

"You don't even need to ask. I had a hamburger earlier."

"You live on fast food."

"I work at a fast job," he replied. "No time for proper meals, now that I'm in a position of responsibility."

She turned and smiled at him. "I was so proud of you for that promotion. You studied hard."

"I might have studied less if I'd realized how much paperwork would be involved," he quipped. "I have eight detectives under me, and I'm responsible for all the major decisions that involve them. Plus I have to coordinate them with other services, work around court dates and emergency assignments . . . Life was a lot easier when I was just a plain detective."

"You love your job, though. That's a bonus."

"It is," he had to agree.

She cut the pie, topped it with a scoop of home-made ice cream and served it to him with his black coffee. She sat down across from him and watched him eat it with real enjoyment, her hands propping up her chin, elbows on the table-cloth.

"You love to cook," he responded.

She nodded. "It isn't an independent woman thing, I know," she said. "I should be designing buildings or running a corporation and yelling at subordinates."

"You should be doing what you want to do," he replied.

"In that case, I am."

"Good cooks are thin on the ground." He finished the pie and leaned back with his coffee cup in his hand, smiling. "Wonderful food!"

"Thanks."

He sipped coffee. "And the best coffee any-where."

"Flattery will get you another slice of pie."

He chuckled. "No more tonight. I'm fine."

"Are you ever going to take a vacation?" she asked.

"Sure," he replied. "I've already arranged to have Christmas Eve off."

She glared at him. "A vacation is longer than one night long."

He frowned. "It is? Are you sure?"

"There's more to life than just work."

"I'll think about that, when I have time."

"Have you watched the news today?" she asked.

"No. Why?"

"They had a special report about violence on the border. It seems that the remaining Fuentes brother sent an armed party over the border to escort a drug shipment and there was a shootout with some border agents."

He grimaced. "An ongoing problem. Nobody knows how to solve it. Bottom line, if people want drugs, somebody's going to supply them. You stop the demand, you stop the supply."

"Good luck with that." She laughed hollowly. "Never going to happen."

"I totally agree."

"Anyway, they mentioned in passing that one of the captured drug runners said that General Emilio Machado was recruiting men for an armed invasion of his former country."

"The Mexican Government, we hear, is not pleased with that development and they're angry at our government because they think we aren't doing enough to stop it."

"Really?" she exclaimed. "What else do you know?"

"Not much, but you can't repeat anything I tell you," he added.

She grinned. "You know I'm as silent as a clam. Come on. Talk."

"Apparently, the State Department sent people into our office," he replied. "We know they talked to our lieutenant, but we don't know what about."

"State Department!"

"They do have their fingers on the pulse of foreign governments," Rick reminded her. "If anybody knows what's really going on, they do."

"I would have thought one of those other government agencies would have been more involved, especially if the general's trying to recruit Americans for a foreign military action," she pondered.

His eyebrows arched.

"Well, it seems logical, doesn't it?" she asked.

"Actually, it does," he agreed. "I know the FBI and the CIA have counterterrorism units that infiltrate groups like that."

"Yes, and some of them die doing it," Barbara recalled. She grimaced. "They say undercover officers in any organization face the highest risks."

"The military also has counterterrorism units,"

he replied. He sipped his cooling coffee. "That must be an interesting sort of job."

"Dangerous."

He smiled. "Of course. But patriotic in the extreme, especially when it comes to foreign operatives trying to undermine democratic interests."

"Doesn't the general's former country have great deposits of oil and natural gas?" she wondered aloud.

"So we hear. It's also in a very strategic location, and the general leans toward capitalism rather than socialism or communism. He's friendly toward the United States."

"A point in his favor. Gracie Pendleton says he sings like an angel," she added with a smile.

"I heard."

"Yes, we had that discussion earlier." She was also remembering another discussion over the phone and her face saddened.

He reached across the table and caught her hand in his. "I really am sorry, Mom," he said gently. "I don't know what came over me. I'm not usually like that."

"No, you're not." She hesitated. She wanted to remark that it wasn't until she asked about the lieutenant giving Gwen a rose that he'd gone ballistic. But in the interests of diplomacy, it was probably wiser to say nothing. She smiled. "How about I warm up that coffee?" she asked instead.

● ● ●

Gwen answered the phone absently, her mind still on the previews of next week's episode of her favorite science fiction show.

"Yes?" she murmured, the hated glasses perched on her nose so that she could actually see the screen of her television.

"Cassaway, anything to report?"

She sat up straighter. "Sir!"

"No need to get uptight. I'm just checking in. The wife and I are on our way to a party, but I wanted to make sure things are progressing well."

"They're going very slowly, sir," she said, curling up in her bare feet and jeans and long-sleeved T-shirt on her sofa. "I'm sorry, I haven't found a diplomatic way to get him talking about the subject and find out what he knows. He doesn't like me. . . ."

"I find that hard to believe, Cassaway. You're a good kid."

She winced at the description.

He cleared his throat. "Sorry. Good woman. I try to be PC, you know, but I come from a different generation. Hard for us old-timers to work well in the new world."

She laughed. "You do fine, sir."

"I know this is a tough assignment," he replied. "But I still think you're the best person for the job. You have a way with people."

"Maybe another type of woman would have

63

been a better choice," she began delicately, "maybe someone more open to flirting, and other things . . ."

"With Marquez? Are you kidding? The guy wrote the book on staunch outlooks! He'd be turned off immediately."

She relaxed a little. "He does seem to be like that."

"Tough, patriotic, a stickler for doing the right thing even when the brass disapproves, and he's got more guts than most men in his position ever develop. Even went right up in the face of a visiting politician to tell him he was putting his foot in his mouth by interfering with a homicide investigation and would regret it when the news media got hold of the story."

She laughed. "I read about that."

"Takes a moral man to be that fearless," her boss continued. "So yes, you're the right choice. You just have to win his confidence. But you're going to have to move a little faster. Things are heating up down in Mexico. We can't be caught lagging when the general makes his move, you know? We have to have intel, we have to be in position to take advantage of any opportunities that present themselves. The general likes us. We want him to continue liking us."

"But we can't help."

He sighed. "No. We can't help. Not obviously. We're in a precarious position these days, and

64

we can't be seen to interfere. But behind the scenes, we can hope to influence people who are in a position to interfere. Marquez is the obvious person to liaison with Machado."

"It's going to be traumatic for him," Gwen said worriedly. "From the little intel I've been able to acquire, he has no idea about his connection to Machado. None at all."

"Pity," he replied. "That's going to makc it harder." He put his hand over the receiver and spoke to someone. "Sorry, my wife's ready to leave. I have to go. Keep me in the loop, and watch your back," he added firmly. "We're trying to get the inside track. There are other people, other operatives, around who would love nothing better than to see us fall on our faces. Other countries would do anything to get a foothold in Barrera. I don't need to tell you who they are, or from what motives they work."

"No, sir, you don't," she agreed. "I'll do the best I can."

"You always do," he said, and there was faint affection in his tone. "Have a good evening. I'll be in touch."

"Yes, sir."

She hung up the cell phone and sat staring at it in her hand. She felt a chill. So much was riding on her ability to be diplomatic and quick and discreet. It wasn't her first difficult assignment; she was not a novice. But until now, she'd had no personal involvement. Her growing feelings for Rick Marquez were complicating things. She shouldn't care so much about how it would hurt him, but she did. If only there was a way, any way, that she could give him a heads-up before the fire hit the fan. Perhaps, she thought, she might be able to work something out if she spoke to Cash Grier. They shared a similar background in covert ops and he knew Marquez. It was worth a try.

So Friday morning, her day off, Gwen got in her small, used foreign car and drove down to Jacobsville, Texas.

Cash Grier met her at the door of his office, smiling, and led her inside, motioning to a chair as he closed the door behind him, locked it and pulled down the shade.

She pursed her lips with a grin. "Unusual precautions," she mused.

He smiled. "I'd put a pillow over the telephone if I thought there might be a wire near it. An ambassador's family habitually did that in Nazi Germany in the 1930s. Even did it in front of the head of the Gestapo once."

Her eyebrows arched as she sat down. "I missed that one."

"New book, about the rise of Hitler, and firsthand American views on the radical changes in society there in the 1930s," he said as he sat

66

down and propped his big booted feet on his desk. "I love World War II history. I could paper my walls with books on the European Theatre and biographies of Patton and Rommel and Montgomery," he added, alluding to three famous World War II generals. "I like to read battle strategies."

"Isn't that a rather strange interest for a guy who worked alone for years, except with an occasional spotter?" she asked, tongue in cheek. It was pretty much an open secret that Grier had been a sniper in his younger days.

He chuckled. "Probably."

"I like history, too," she replied. "But I lean more toward political history."

"Which brings us to the question of why you're here," he replied and smiled.

She drew in a long breath and leaned forward. "I have a very unpleasant assignment. It involves Rick Marquez."

He nodded and his face sobered. "I know. I still have high-level contacts in your agency."

"He has no idea what's about to go down," she said. "I've argued with my boss until I'm blue in the face, but they won't let me give Marquez even a hint."

"I think his mother knows," he said. "She asked me about it. She overheard some visitors from D.C. talking about connections."

"Do you think she's told him anything?"

"She might know that his mother was romantically involved with Machado at some point. But she wouldn't know the rest. His mother was very close about her private life. Only one or two people even knew what happened." He grimaced. "The problem is that one of the people involved had a cousin who married a high-level agent in D.C., and he spilled his guts. That started this whole chain of events."

"Hard to keep a secret like that, especially one that would have been so obvious." She frowned. "Rick's stepfather must have known. From what little information I've been able to gather about his past, he and his stepfather didn't get along at all."

"The man beat him," Grier said harshly. "A real jewel of a human being. It's one reason Rick had so many problems as a kid. He was in trouble constantly right up until the wreck that killed his mother and stepfather. It was a tragedy that produced golden results. Barbara took him in, straightened him out and put him on a path that turned him into an exemplary citizen. Without her influence . . ." He spread his hands expressively.

Gwen stared at her scuffed black loafers. Idly, she noticed that they needed some polish. She dressed casually, but she liked to be as neat as possible. One day her real identity would come out, and she didn't want to give the agency a black eye by being slack in her grooming habits.

"You want me to tell him, don't you?" Grier asked.

She looked up. "You know him a lot better than I do. He's my boss, figuratively speaking. He doesn't like me very much, either."

"He might like you more if you'd wear your damned glasses and stop tripping over evidence in crime scenes," he said, pursing his lips. "Alice Mayfield Jones Fowler, who works in the Crime Scene Unit in San Antonio, was eloquent about the close call."

Gwen flushed. "Yes, I know." She pushed the hated glasses up on her nose, where they'd slipped. "I'm wearing my glasses now."

"I didn't mean to be critical," he said, noting her discomfort. "You're a long way from the homicide detective you started out to be," he added. "I know it's a pain, trying to relearn procedure on the fly."

"It really is," she said. "My credentials did stand up to a background check, thank goodness, but I feel like I'm walking on eggshells. I let slip that my job involved a lot of traveling and Marquez wondered why, since I was apparently working for Atlanta Homicide."

"Ouch," he said.

"I have to remember that I've never been out of the country. It's pretty hard, living two lives."

"I haven't forgotten that aspect of government work," he agreed. "It's why I never had

69

much of a personal life, until Tippy came along."

Everybody local knew that Tippy had been a famous model, and then actress. She and Cash had a rocky trip to the altar, but they had a little girl almost two years old and it was rumored that they wanted another child.

"You got lucky," she said.

He shrugged. "I guess I did. I never could see myself settling down in a small town and becoming a family man. But now, it's second nature. Tris is growing by leaps and bounds. She has red hair, and green eyes, like her mama's."

Gwen noted the color photo on his desk, with himself and Tippy, with Tris and a boy who looked to be in his early teens. "Is that Tippy's brother?" she asked, indicating the photo.

"Rory," he agreed. "He's fourteen." He shook his head. "Time flies."

"It seems to." She leaned back again. "I miss my dad. He's been overseas for a long time, although he's coming back soon for a talk with some very high-level people in D.C. and rumors are flying. Rick Marquez has no idea what sort of back-ground I come from."

"Another shock in store for him," he added. "You should tell him."

"I can't. That would lead to other questions." She sighed. "I'd love to meet my dad at the air-port when he flies in. We've had a rough six months since my brother, Larry, died overseas.

Dad still mourns my mother, and she's been gone for years. I miss her, too."

"I heard about your brother from a friend in the agency. I'm truly sorry." His dark eyes narrowed. "No other siblings?"

She shook her head.

"My mother's gone, too. But my dad's still alive, and I have three brothers," he replied with a smile. "My older brother, Garon, is SAC at the San Antonio FBI office."

"I've met him. He's very nice." She studied his face. He was a striking man, even with hair that was going silver at the temples. His dark eyes were piercing and steady. He looked intimidating sitting behind a desk. She could only imagine how intimidating he'd look on the job.

"What are you thinking so hard about?" he queried.

"That I never want to break the law in your town." She chuckled.

He grinned. "Thanks. I try to perfect a suitably intimidating demeanor on the job."

"It's quite good."

He sighed. "I'll talk to Marquez's mother and plant clues. I'll do it discreetly. Nobody will ever know that you mentioned it to me, I promise."

"Least of all my boss, who'd have me on security details for the rest of my professional life," she said with a laugh. "I don't doubt he'd have me transferred as liaison to a police

71

department for real, where he'd make sure I was assigned to duty at school crossings."

"Hey, now, that's a nice job," he protested. "My patrolmen fight over that one." He said it tongue in cheek. "In fact, the last one enjoyed it so much that he transferred to the fire department. It seems that a first-grader kicked him in the leg, repeatedly."

Her fine eyebrows arched. "Why?"

"He told the kid to stay in the crosswalk. Seems the kid had a real attitude problem. The teachers couldn't deal with him, so they finally called us, after the kicking incident. I took the kid home, in the patrol car, and had a long talk with his mother."

"Oh, dear."

His face was grim. "She's a single parent, living alone, no family anywhere, and this kid is one step away from juvy," he added, referencing the juvenile justice system. "He's six years old," he said heavily, "and he already has a record for disobedience and detention at his school."

"They put little kids in detention in grammar school?" she exclaimed.

"Figure of speech. They call it time-out and he sits in the library. Last time he had to go there, he stood on one of the library tables and recited the Bill of Rights to the head librarian."

Her eyes widened in amusement. "Not only a troublemaker, but brilliant to boot."

He nodded. "Everybody's hoping his poor mother will marry a really tough hombre who can control him before he does something unforgivable and gets an arrest record."

She laughed. "The things I miss because I never married," she mused, shaking her head. "It's not an incentive to become a parent."

"On the other end of the spectrum, there's Tippy and me," he replied with a smile. "I love being a dad."

"It suits you," she said.

She got to her feet. "Well, I have to get back to San Antonio. If Sergeant Marquez asks, I had to talk to you about a case, okay?"

"In fact, we really do have a case that might connect," he said surprisingly. "Sit back down and I'll tell you about it."

CHAPTER 4

Sergeant Marquez came into the office two days later, looking grim. He motioned to Gwen, indicated a chair and closed the door.

She remembered her trip to Cash Grier's office, and wondered if Grier had had time to talk to her superior officer's mother and the information had tricked down.

"The cold case squad has a job for us," he said as he sat down, too.

"What sort of job?"

"They dug up an old murder. It was committed back in 2002 and a man went to prison on evidence largely given by one person. Now it seems the person who gave evidence has been arrested and convicted for a similar crime. They want to know if we can find a connection."

"Well, by chance, that was the case I just spoke to Chief Grier about down in Jacobsville," she told him, happy that she could make a legitimate connection to her impromptu trip out of town. "He has an officer who knew the prisoner's family and could place the man at a party during the murder."

"Did he give evidence?" he asked.

She shook her head. "He was never called to testify," she said. "Nobody knows why."

"Isn't that interesting."

"Very. So the cold case squad wants us to wear out some shoe leather on their behalf?"

He grimaced. "They have plenty of manpower, but they've got two people out sick, one just transferred to the white collar crime unit and their sergeant said they don't want to let this case get buried. Especially not when a similar crime was just committed here. Your case. The college woman who was murdered. It needs investigation, and they don't have enough people." He smiled. "Besides, there's the issue of not stepping on the toes of another unit's investigation."

"I can understand that."

"So, we'll see if we can make a connection, based on available evidence. I'm assigning you as lead detective on this case, as well as on the college freshman murder. Find a connection. Catch the perp. Make me proud."

She grinned at him. "Actually, that might be possible. I just got some new information from running a check on the photo of that odd man in the murder victim's camera. The one I mentioned to you?"

"Yes, I recall that."

She pulled up a file on her phone. "This is him. I used face recognition software to pick him out." She showed him the mug shot on her phone. "The perp. His name is Mickey Dunagan. He has a rap sheet. It's a long one. He's been prosecuted in two aggravated assault cases, never convicted. Here's the clincher. He has a thing for young college girls. He was arrested for attempted assault a few months ago, on a girl who went to the same college as our victim. I have a detective from our unit en route to question her today, and we're interviewing people at the apartment complex about the man in the photograph. If his DNA is on file, and I'm betting it is since he's served time during his trials, and there's enough DNA from the crime scene to type and match . . ."

"Good work!" he said fervently.

She grinned. "Thanks, sir."

"I wish we could get ironclad evidence that he killed the victim." He grimaced. "Not that ironclad evidence ever got a conviction when some silver-tongued gung-ho public defender got the bit between his teeth."

"Impressive mixing of metaphors, sir," she murmured dryly.

He actually made a face at her. "Correct my grammar, get stakeout duty for the next two months."

"I would never do that!" she protested with wicked, twinkling eyes.

He smiled back. She was very pretty when she

smiled. Her mouth was full and lush and sensuous . . .

He sat back in his chair and forced himself not to notice that. "Get busy."

"I'll get on it right now."

"Just out of curiosity, who was the officer who could place the convicted murderer at a party when the other murder was committed?"

"Officer Dan Travis," she said. "He's at the Jacobsville Police Department. I'm going to drive down and talk to him tomorrow." She checked the notes on her phone. "Dunagan was arrested for assault by a patrolman in South Division named Dave Harris. I'm going to talk to him afterward. He might remember something that would be helpful."

"Good. Keep me in the loop."

"I will." She got up and started for the door.

"Cassaway."

She turned at the door. "Sir?"

His dark eyes narrowed. He seemed deep in thought. He was. He had a strange sense that she knew something important that she was hiding from him. He read body language very well after his long years in law enforcement. He'd once tripped a bank robber up when he noticed the man's behavior and deliberately engaged him in conversation. During the conversation, he'd gotten close enough to see the gun the man was holding under his long coat. Rick had quickly subdued him, cuffed him, and taken him in for questioning. The impromptu encounter had solved a whole string of unsolved bank robberies for the cold case unit, and their sergeant, Dave Murphy, had taken Rick out to lunch in appreciation for the help.

"Sir?" Gwen prompted when he didn't reply.

He sat up straight. His eyes narrowed further as he stared at her. She was almost twitching. "What do you know," he said softly, "that you aren't telling me?"

Her face flushed. "No . . . nothing. I mean, there's . . . nothing," she faltered, and could have bitten her tongue for making things worse.

"You need to think about your priorities," he said curtly.

She drew in a long breath. "Believe me, I am."

He grimaced and waved his hand in her direction. "Get to work."

"Yes, sir."

She almost ran out of the office. She was flushed and unsettled. Lieutenant Hollister met her in the hall, and frowned.

"What's up?" he asked gently.

She bit her lip. "Nothing, sir," she said. She drew in a long breath. She wanted, so badly, to tell somebody what was going on.

Hollister's black eyes narrowed. "Come into my office for a minute."

He led her back the way she'd come, past a

startled Marquez, who watched the couple go into the lieutenant's office with an expression that was hard to classify.

"Sit down," Hollister said. He went behind his desk and swung up his long, powerful legs, propping immaculate black boots on the desk. He crossed his arms and leaned back precariously in his chair. "Talk."

She shifted restlessly. "I know something about Sergeant Marquez that I'm not supposed to discuss with anybody."

He lifted a thick blond eyebrow. He even smiled. "I know what it is."

Her green eyes widened.

"The suits who came to see me earlier in the week were feds," he said. "I know who you really are, and what's going on." He sighed. "I want to tell Marquez, too, but my hands are tied."

"I went to see Cash Grier," she said. "He's out of the loop. He can't do anything directly, but he might be able to let something slip at Barbara's Café in Jacobsville. That would at least prepare Sergeant Marquez for what's about to go down."

"Nothing can prepare a man for that sort of revelation, believe me." His eyes narrowed even more. "They want Marquez as a liaison, don't they?"

She nodded. "He'd be the best man for the job. But he's going to be very upset at first and he may refuse to do anything."

"That's a risk they're willing to take. They don't dare interfere directly, not in the current political climate," he added. "Frankly, I'd just go tell him."

"Would you?" she asked, and smiled.

He laughed deeply and then he shook his head. "Actually, no, I wouldn't. I'm too handsome to spend time in prison. There would be riots. I'd be so much in demand as somebody's significant other."

She laughed, too. She hadn't realized he had a sense of humor. Her face flushed. She looked very pretty.

He cocked his head. "You could just ask Marquez to the ballet and tell him yourself."

"My boss would have me hung in Hogan's Alley up at the FBI Academy with a placard around my neck as a warning to other loose-lipped agents," she told him.

He grinned. "I'd come cut you down, Cassaway. I get along well with the feds. But I'm not prejudiced. I also get along with mercenaries."

"There's a rumor that you used to be one," she fished.

His face closed up, although he was still smiling. "How about that?"

She didn't comment.

He swung his long legs off the desk and stood up. "Let me know how it goes," he said. He walked her to the door. "It's not a bad idea, about asking him to the ballet. He loves ballet.

He usually goes alone. He can't get girlfriends."

"Why not?" she asked. She cleared her throat. "I mean, he's rather attractive."

"He wears a gun."

"So do you," she pointed out, indicating the holster. "In fact, we all wear them."

"True, but he likes women who don't," he replied. "And they don't like men who wear guns. He doesn't date colleagues, he says. But you might be able to change his mind."

"Fat chance." She sighed. "He doesn't like me."

"Go solve that murder for the cold case unit, and they'll lobby him for you," he teased.

"How do you know about that?" she asked, surprised.

"I'm the lieutenant," he pointed out. "I know everything," he added smugly.

She laughed. She was still laughing when she walked down the corridor.

Rick heard her from inside his office. He threw a scratch pad across the room and knocked the trash can across the floor with it. Then he grimaced, in case anybody heard and asked what was going on. He couldn't have told them. He didn't know himself why he was behaving so out of character.

The man Gwen was tracking in her semiofficial disguise was an unpleasant, slinky individual who had a rap sheet that read like a short story.

She'd gone down to Jacobsville and interviewed Officer Dan Travis. He seemed a decent sort of person, and he could swear that the man who was arrested for the murder was at a holiday party with him, and had never even stepped outside. He had told the assistant DA, but the attorney refused to entertain evidence he considered hearsay. Travis gave her the names of two other people she could contact, who would verify the information. She took notes and arranged for a deposition to be taken from him.

Her next stop was Patrol South Division, in San Antonio, to talk to the arresting officer who'd taken Dunagan in for the attempted assault on a college woman a few months ago, Dave Harris. He was working that day, but was working a wreck when she phoned him. So she arranged to meet him for lunch at a nearby fast food joint.

They sat together over hamburgers and fries and soft drinks, attracting attention with his uniform and her pistol and badge, conspicuously displayed.

"We're being watched," she said in a dramatic tone, indicating two young women at a nearby booth.

"Oh, that's just Joan and Shirley," he said. He looked toward the women, waved and grinned. One of them flushed and almost knocked over her drink. He was blond and blue-eyed, nicely built, and quite handsome. He was also single.

"Joan's sweet on me," he added in a whisper. "They know I always eat here, so they come by for lunch. They work at the print shop downtown. Joan's a graphic artist. Very talented."

"Nice," she murmured, biting into the burger.

"Why are you doing a cold case?" he asked as he finished his salad and sipped black coffee.

"It ties in with a current one we're working on," she said, and related what Cash Grier had told her.

His dark eyebrows arched. "They never called a prime witness in the case?"

"Strange, isn't it?" she agreed. "That would be grounds for a mistrial, I'd think, but I'll need to talk to the city attorney's office first. The man who was convicted has been in prison for almost a year."

"Shame, if he's innocent," the patrolman replied.

"I know. Fortunately, such things don't happen often."

"What about the suspect in your current case?"

"A nasty bit of work," she replied. "I can place him at the scene of the crime, and if there's enough trace evidence to do a DNA profile, I think I can connect him with it. Her neighbors reported seeing him around her apartment the morning before the murder. If he's guilty, I don't want him to slip through the cracks on my watch, especially since Sergeant Marquez assigned me to the case as chief investigator."

"Really? How many other people are helping you with the case?"

"Let's see, right now, there's me and one other detective that I borrowed to help question witnesses."

He sighed. "Budget issues again?"

"Afraid so. I can manage. If I need help, the cold case unit will lend me somebody."

"Nice group, that cold case unit."

She smiled. "I think so, too."

"Now about the perp," he added, leaning forward. "This is how it went down."

He described the scene of the assault where he'd arrested Dunagan, the persons involved, the witnesses and his own part in the arrest. Gwen made notes on her phone and saved the file.

"That's a big help," she told him. "Thanks."

He smiled. "You're very welcome." He checked his watch. "I have to get back on patrol. Was there any other information you needed?"

"Nothing I can't find in the file. I appreciate the summary of the case, and your thoughts on it. That really helps."

"You're welcome. Any time."

"Shame about the latest victim," she added as they got up and headed to the trash bin with their trays. "She was very pretty. Her neighbors said she went out of her way to help people in need." She glanced at him. "We had one of your fellow officers on stakeout with us the other night. Sims."

He paused as he dumped the paper waste and placed the tray in its stack on the refuse container top. "He's not our usual sort of patrol officer."

"What do you mean?" she asked, frowning.

"I really can't say anything. It's just that he has an interesting background. There are people in high positions with influence," he added. He smiled. "But he's not my problem. I think you'll do well in the homicide unit. You've got a knack for sorting things out, and you're thorough. Good luck on the case."

"Thanks. Thanks a lot."

He smiled. "You're welcome."

She drove back to the office with her brain spinning. What she'd learned was very helpful. She might crack the case, which would certainly give her points with Rick Marquez. But there was still the problem of what she knew and couldn't tell him. She only hoped that Cash Grier would be able to break some ground with her sergeant.

Cash Grier had a thick ham sandwich with home-made fries and black coffee and then asked for a slice of Barbara's famous apple pie and home-made ice cream.

She served it with a grin. "Don't eat too much of this," she cautioned. "It's very fattening." She was teasing, because he was still as trim as men ten years his junior, and nicely muscled.

He pursed his lips and his black eyes twinkled. "As you can see, I'm running to fat."

She laughed. "That'll be the day."

He studied her quietly. "Can you sit down for a minute?"

She looked around. The lunchtime rush was over and there were only a couple of cowboys and an elderly couple in the café. "Sure." She sat down across from him. "What can I do for you?"

He sipped coffee. "I've been enlisted to get some information to your son without telling him any-thing."

She blinked. "That's a conundrum."

"Isn't it?" He put down the coffee cup and smiled. "You're a very intelligent woman. You must have some suspicions about his family history."

"Thanks for the compliment. And yes, I have a lot." She studied his hard face. "I overheard some feds who ate here talking about Dolores Ortíz and her connection to General Machado. Dolores worked for me just briefly. She was Rick's birth mother."

"Rick's stepfather was a piece of work," he said coldly. "I've heard plenty about him. He mistreated livestock and was fired for it on the Ballenger feedlot. Gossip is that he did the same to his stepson."

Her face tautened. "When I first adopted him, I lifted my hand to smooth back his hair—you know, that thing mothers do when they feel affectionate. He stiffened and cringed." Her eyes were sad. "That's when I first knew that there was a reason for his bad behavior. I've never hit him. But someone did."

"His stepfather," Grier asserted. "With assorted objects, including, once, a leather whip."

"So that's where he got those scars on his back," she faltered. "I asked, but he would never talk about it."

"It's a blow to a man's pride to have something like that done to him," he said coldly. "Jackson should have been sent to prison on a charge of child abuse."

"I do agree." She hesitated. "Rick's last name is Marquez. But Dolores said that was a name she had legally drawn up when Rick was seven. I never understood."

"She didn't dare put his real father's name on a birth certificate," he replied. "Even at the time, his dad was in trouble with the law in Mexico. She didn't want him to know about Rick. And, later, she had good reason to keep the secret. She married Craig Jackson to give Rick a settled home. She didn't know what sort of man he was until it was too late," he added coldly. "He knew who Rick's real father was and threatened to make it public if Dolores left him. So she stayed and Rick paid for her silence."

Barbara was feeling uncomfortable. "Would

his real father happen to be an exiled South American dictator, by any chance?"

Grier nodded.

"Oh, boy."

"And nobody can tell him, because a certain federal agency is hoping to talk him into being a go-between for them, to help coax Machado into a comfortable trade agreement with our country when he gets back into power. Which he certainly will," he added quietly. "The thug who took over his government has human rights advocates bristling all over the world. He's tortured people, murdered dissenters, closed down public media outlets . . . In general, he's done everything possible to outrage anyone who believes in democracy. At the same time, he's pocketing money from sources of revenue and buying himself every rich man's perk that he can dream up. He's got several Rolls-Royce cars, assorted beautiful women, houses in most affluent European cities and his own private jet to take him to them. He doesn't govern so much as he flaunts his position. Workers are starving and farmers are being forced to grow drug crops to support his extravagant lifestyle." He shook his head. "I've seen dictators come and go, but that man needs a little lead in his diet."

She knew what he was alluding to. "Any plans going to take care of that?" she mused.

"Don't look at me," he warned. "I'm retired. I have a family to think about."

"Eb Scott might have a few people who would be interested in the work."

"Yes, he might, but the general isn't lacking for good help." He glanced up as one of Barbara's workers came, smiling, to refill his coffee cup. "Thanks."

She grinned. "You're welcome. Boss lady, you want some?"

Barbara shook her head. "Thanks, Bess, I'm already flying on a caffeine high."

"Okay."

"So who has to do the dirty work and tell Rick the truth?" Barbara asked.

Grier didn't speak. He just smiled at her.

"Oh, darn it, I won't do it!"

"There's nobody else. The feds have forbidden their agents to tip him off. His lieutenant knows, but he's been gagged, too."

"Then how in the world do they expect him to find out? Why won't they just tell him?"

"Because he might get mad at them for being the source of the revelation and refuse to cooperate. And there isn't anybody else they can find to do the job of contacting Machado."

"They could ask Grange," Barbara said stubbornly. "He's already working for the general, isn't he?"

"Grange doesn't know."

"Why me?" she groaned. "He'll be furious!"

"Yes, but you're his mother and he loves you," he replied. "If you tell him, he'll get over it. He might even be receptive to helping the feds. If they tell him, he'll hold a grudge and they'll never find anyone halfway suitable to do the job."

She was silent. She stared at the festive table-cloth worriedly.

"It will be all right," he assured her gently.

She looked up. "We've already had a disagreement recently."

"You have? Why?" he asked, surprised, because Rick's devotion to his adopted mother was quite well-known locally.

She grimaced. "His lieutenant gave the new detective, Gwen Cassaway, a rose, and I mentioned it in a teasing way. He went ballistic and I hung up on him. He won't admit it, but I think he's got a case on Gwen."

"Well!" he mused.

That was a new and interesting proposition. "Couldn't she tell him?" she asked hopefully.

"She's been cautioned not to."

She sighed. "Darn. Does everybody know?"

"Rick doesn't."

"I noticed."

"So you have to tell him. And soon."

"Or what?"

He leaned forward. "Or six government agencies will send operatives down here to disparage your apple pie and accuse you of subverting government policy by using organic products in your kitchen."

She burst out laughing. "Yes, I did hear that a SWAT team of federal agents raided a farm that was selling unpasteurized milk. Can you believe that? In our country, in this day and time, with all the real problems going on, we have to send armed operatives against people living in a natural harmony with the earth?"

"You're kidding!" he exclaimed.

"I wish I was," she replied. "I guess we're all going to be force-fed Genetically Modified Organisms from now on."

He burst out laughing. "You need to stop hanging out on those covert websites."

"I can't. I'd never know what was really going on in the world, like us having bases on the moon."

He rolled his eyes. "I have to get back to work." He stood up. "You'll tell him, then."

She stood up, too. "Do I have a choice?"

"You could move to Greenland and change your name."

She made a face at him. "That's no choice. Although I would love to visit Greenland. They have snow."

"So do we, occasionally."

"They have lots of snow. Enough to make many snowmen. South Texas isn't famous for that."

"The pie was great, by the way."

She smiled. "Thanks. I do my best."

"I'd have to leave town if you ever closed up," he told her. "I can't live in a town that doesn't have the best food in Texas."

"That will get you extra ice cream on your next slice of apple pie!" she promised him with a grin.

But she wasn't grinning when she went home. It disturbed her that she was going to have to tell her son something that would devastate him. He wasn't going to be pleased. Other than that, she didn't know what the outcome would be. But Grier was right about one thing; it was better that the information came from his mother rather than from some bureaucrat or federal agent who had no personal involvement with Rick and didn't care how the news affected him. It did make her feel good that so far, they hadn't blurted it out. By hesitating, they did show some compassion.

Rick went to his mother's home tired. It had been a long day of meetings and more meetings, with a workshop on gun safety occasioned by the accidental discharge of a pistol by one of the patrol officers. The bullet went into the asphalt but fortunately didn't ricochet and hit anything, or anyone. The officer was disciplined but the chain of command saw an opportunity to emphasize gun safety and they took it. The moral of the story was that even experienced officers could mishandle a gun.

Privately, Marquez wondered how Officer Sims ever got through the police academy, because he was the officer involved. The same guy who'd gone on stakeout with him and Cassaway. He didn't think a lot of the young man's ethics and he'd heard that Sims had an uncle high up in the chain of command who made sure he kept his job. It was disturbing.

"You look worn-out," Barbara said gently. "Come sit down and I'll put supper on the table."

"It's late," he commented, noting his watch.

"We can have supper at midnight," she teased. "Nobody's watching. I'll even pull down the shades if it makes you happy."

He laughed and hugged her. "You're a treasure, Mom. I'll never marry unless I can find a girl like you."

"That's sweet. Thanks."

She started heating up roast beef and buttered rolls, topping off his plate with homemade potato salad. She put the plate in front of him. "Thank goodness for microwave ovens." She laughed. "The cook's best friend."

"This is delicious." He closed his eyes, savoring every bite. "I had a sandwich for lunch and I only had time to eat half of it between meetings."

"I didn't even eat lunch," she said, dipping into her own roast beef.

"Why not?"

"I had a talk with Cash Grier and afterward I lost my appetite."

He stopped eating and stared at her with narrowed eyes. "What did he tell you?"

"Something everybody knows and nobody has the guts to tell you, my darling," she said, stiffening herself mentally. "I have some very unpleasant news."

He put down his fork. "You've got cancer." His face paled. "That's it, isn't it? You should have told me . . . !"

He got up and hugged her. "We'll get through it together. I'll never leave your side . . ."

She pulled back, flattered. "I'm fine," she said. "I don't have anything fatal. That isn't what I meant. It's about you. And your real father."

He blinked. "My real father died not long after I was born . . ."

She took a deep breath. "Rick, your real father is across the border in Mexico amassing a private army in preparation for invading a South American country."

He sat down, hard. His light olive complexion was suddenly very pale. All the gossip and secrecy suddenly made sense. The feds were all over his office, not because they were working on shared cases, but because of Rick.

"My father is General Emilio Machado," he said with sudden realization.

CHAPTER 5

"My father is a South American dictator," Rick repeated, almost in shock.

"I'm afraid so." Barbara pulled up a chair facing him and held his hand that was resting on the table. "They made me tell you. Nobody else wanted to. I'm so sorry."

"But my mother said my father was dead," he repeated blankly.

"She only wanted to protect you. Machado was in trouble with the Mexican authorities when he lived in the country because he was opposed to foreign interests trying to take over key industries where he lived. He organized protests even when he was in his teens. He was a natural leader. Later, Dolores didn't dare tell you because Machado was the head of a fairly well-known international paramilitary group and that would have made you a target for any extremist with a grudge. He was in the news a lot when you were a child."

"Does he know?" Rick persisted. "Does he know about me?"

Barbara bit her lower lip. "No. She never told

him." She sighed. "After Cash told me who your father was, I remembered something that Dolores told me. She said your father was only fourteen when he fathered you. She was older, seventeen, and there was no chance that her family would have let her marry him. She wanted you very much. So she had you, and never even told her parents who the father was. She kept her secret. At least, until she married your stepfather. Cash said that your stepfather got the truth out of her and used it to keep her with him. She didn't dare protest or he'd have made your real identity known. A true charmer," she added sarcastically.

"My stepfather was a sadist," he said quietly. "I've never spoken of him to you. But he made my life hell, and my mother's as well. I got in trouble with the law on purpose. I thought maybe somebody would check out my home life and see the truth and help us. But nobody ever did. Not until you came along and offered my mother work."

"I tried to help," she agreed. "Dolores liked cooking for me, but your stepfather didn't like her having friends or any interest outside of him. He was insanely jealous."

"He also couldn't keep a job. Money was tight. You used to sneak me food," he recalled with a warm smile. "You even came to visit me in the detention center. My mother appreciated that. My stepfather wouldn't let her come."

"I knew that. I did what I could. I tried to get our police chief at the time to investigate, but he was the sort of man who didn't want to rock the boat." She laughed. "Can you imagine Cash Grier turning a blind eye to something like that?"

"He'd have had my stepfather pilloried in the square." Rick smiled, then sobered. "My father is a dictator," he repeated again. It was hard to believe. He'd spent his whole life certain that his biological father was long dead.

"A deposed dictator," Barbara corrected. "His country is going to the dogs under its new administration. People are dying. He wants to accomplish a military coup, but he needs all the help he can get. Which brings us to our present situation," she added. "A paramilitary group is going down to Barrera with him, including some of Eb Scott's guys, some Europeans, one African merc and with ex-army Major Winslow Grange, Jason Pendleton's foreman on his Comanche Wells ranch, to lead them."

"All that firepower and the government hasn't noticed?"

"It wouldn't do them a lot of good. Machado's in Mexico, just over the border," Barbara said. "They can't mount an invasion to stop him. But they can try to find a way to be friendly without overt aid."

"Ah. I see. I'm the goat."

She blinked. "Excuse me?"

"They're going to tether me out to attract the puma."

"Puma." She laughed. "Funny, but one of my customers said that's what the local population calls 'El General.' They say he's cunning and dangerous like a cat, but that he can purr when he wants to." Her face softened. "For a dictator, he's held in high esteem by most democracies. He's intelligent, kind, he reveres women and he isn't afraid to fight for justice."

"Does he wear a red cape?" Rick murmured.

She shook her head. "Sorry."

"Who's in on this?" he asked narrowly. "Does my lieutenant know?"

"Yes," she said. "And there's a covert operative somewhere in your organization," she added. "I got that tidbit from a patrol officer who has a friend on the force in San Antonio. A guy named Sims."

"Sims." His face closed up. "He's got connections. And he's a total ethical wipeout. I hate having a guy like that on the force. He got careless with a pistol and almost shot himself in the foot. He's the reason we just had a gun safety workshop."

"Learning gun safety is not a bad thing."

He sighed. "I know." He was trying to adjust to the shock of his parentage. "Why didn't my mother tell me?" he burst out.

"She was trying to protect you. I'm certain that

she would have told you eventually," she added. "She just didn't have time before she died."

He grimaced. "What am I supposed to do now, walk over the border, find the general and say, hey, guess what, I'm your kid?"

"I don't really think that would be wise," she replied. "I'm not sure he'd believe it in the first place. Would you?"

"Now there's a question." He leaned back in the chair, his dark eyes focused on the tablecloth. "I suppose I could have a DNA profile done. There's a private company that can at least rule out paternity by blood type. If mine is compatible with the general's, it might help convince him . . . Wait a minute," he added coldly. "Why the hell should I care?"

"Because he's your father, Rick," she said gently. "Even though he doesn't know."

"And the government's only purpose in telling me is to help reunite us," he returned angrily.

"Well, no, they want someone to convince the general to make a trade agreement with us once he's back in power. They're certain that he will be, which is why they want you to make friends with him."

"I'm sure he'll be overjoyed to know he has a grown son who's a cop," he said coldly. "Especially since he's wanted by our government for kidnapping."

She leaned forward with her chin resting in her

hands, propped by her elbows. "You could arrest him," she pointed out. "And then befriend him in jail. Like the mouse that took the thorn out of the lion's paw and became its friend."

He made a face at her. "I can't walk across the border and arrest anyone. I might have been born in Mexico, but I'm an American citizen. And I did it the hard way," he added firmly. "Legally."

She grimaced.

"Sorry," he said after a minute. "I know you sympathize with all the people hiding out here who couldn't afford to wait for permission. In some of their countries, they could be killed just for paying too much attention to the wrong people."

"It's very bad in some Central American states," she pointed out.

"It's very bad anywhere on our border."

"And getting worse."

He got up and poured himself another cup of coffee. His big hand rested on the coffeemaker as he switched it off. "Who's the mole in my office?"

"I honestly don't know," she replied. "I only know that Sims told his friend, Cash Grier's patrolman, about it. He said it was someone from a federal agency, working undercover."

"I wonder how Sims knew."

"Maybe he's the mole," she teased.

"Unlikely. Most feds have too much respect for the law to abuse it. Sims actually suggested that we confiscate a six-pack of beer from a convenience store as evidence in some pretended case and threaten the clerk with jail if he told on us."

"Good grief! And he works for the police?" she exclaimed, horrified.

"Apparently," he replied. "I didn't like what he said, and I told him so. He seemed repentant, but I'm not sure he really was. Cocky kid. Real attitude problem."

"Doesn't that sound familiar?" she asked the room at large.

"I never suggested breaking the law after I went through the academy and swore under oath to uphold it," he replied.

"Are you sure you didn't overreact, my darling?" she asked gently.

"If I did, so did Cassaway. She was hotter under the collar than I was." He laughed shortly. "And then she beat the lieutenant on the firing range and he let out a bad word. She marched right up to him and said she was offended and he shouldn't talk that way around her." He glanced at her ruefully. "Hence, the rose."

"Oh. An apology." She looked disappointed. "Your lieutenant is very attractive," she mused. "And eligible. I thought he might find Miss Cassaway interesting. Or something."

"Maybe he does," he said vaguely. "God knows why. She's good with a gun, I'll give her that, but she's a walking disaster in other ways. How she ever got a job with the police, I'll never know." He didn't like talking about Cassaway and the lieutenant. It got under his skin, for reasons he couldn't understand.

"She sounds very nice to me."

"Everybody sounds nice to you," he replied. He smiled at her. "You could find one good thing to say about the devil, Mom. You look for the best in people."

"You look for the worst," she pointed out.

He shrugged. "That's my job."

He was thoughtful, and morose. She felt even more guilty when she saw how disturbed he really was.

"I wish there had been some other way to handle this," she muttered angrily. "I hate being made the fall guy."

"Hey, I'm not mad at you," he said, and bent to kiss her hair. "I just . . . don't know what to do." He sighed.

" 'When in doubt, don't,' " she quoted. She frowned. "Who said that?"

"Beats me, but it's probably good advice." He put down his cooling coffee and stretched, yawning. "I'm beat. Too many late nights finishing paperwork and going on stakeouts. I'm going to bed. I'll decide what to do in the morning. Maybe it will come to me in a dream or something," he added.

"Maybe it will. I'm just sorry I had to be the one to tell you."

"I'll get used to the idea," he assured her. "I just need a little time."

She nodded.

But time was in short supply. Two days later, a tall, elegant man with dark hair and eyes, wearing a visitor's tag but no indication of his identity, walked into Rick's office and closed the door.

"I need to talk to you," he said.

Rick stared at him. "Do I know you?" he asked after a minute, because the man seemed vaguely familiar.

"You should," he replied with a grin. "But it's been a while since we caught Fuentes and his boys in the drug sting in Jacobsville. I'm Rodrigo Ramirez. DEA."

"I knew you looked familiar!" Rick got up and shook the other man's hand. "Yes, it has been a while. You and your wife bought a house here last year."

He nodded. "I work out of San Antonio DEA now instead of Houston, and she works for the local prosecutor, Blake Kemp, in Jacobsville. With her high blood pressure, I'd rather she stayed at home, but she said she'd do it when I did it." He shrugged. "Neither of us was willing to try to change professions at this late date. So we deal with the occasional problem."

"Are you mixed up in the Barrera thing as well?" Rick asked curiously.

"In a way. I'm related, distantly, to a high official in Mexico," he said. "It gives me access to some privileged information." He hesitated. "I don't know how much they've told you."

Rick motioned Ramirez into a chair and sat down behind his desk. "I know that El General has a son who's a sergeant with San Antonio P.D.," he said sarcastically.

"So you know."

"My mother told me. They wanted me to know, but nobody had the guts to just say it," he bit off.

"Yes, well, that could have been a big problem. Depending on how you were told, and by whom. They were afraid of alienating you."

"I don't see what help I'm going to be," Rick said irritably. "I didn't know my biological father was still alive, much less who he was. The general, I'm told, has no clue that I even exist. I doubt he'd take my word for it."

"So do I. Sometimes government agencies are a little thin on common sense," he added. He crossed his elegant long legs. "I've been elected, you might say, to do the introductions, by my cousin."

"Your cousin . . . ?"

"He's the president of Mexico."

"Well, damn!"

Ramirez smiled. "That's what I said when he told me to do it."

"Sorry."

"No problem. It seems we're both stuck with doing something that goes against the grain. I think the general is going to react very badly. I wish there was someone who could talk to him for us."

"Like my mother talked to me for the feds?" he mused.

"Exactly."

Rick frowned. "You know, Gracie Pendleton got along quite well with him. She refused to even think of pressing charges. She was asked, in case we could talk about extradition of Machado with the Mexican government. She said no."

"I heard. She's my sister-in-law, although she's not related to my wife. Don't even ask," he added, waving his hand. "It's far too complicated to explain."

"I won't. But I remember Glory very well," he reminded Ramirez. "Cash Grier and I taught her how to shoot a pistol without destroying cars in the parking lot," he added with a grin.

Ramirez laughed. "So you did." He sobered. "Gracie might be willing to speak to the general, if we could get word to him," Ramirez said.

"We had a guy in jail here who was one of the higher-ups in the Fuentes organization. He's going on probation tomorrow."

"An opportunity." Ramirez chuckled.

"Apparently, a timely one. I'll ask him if he'd have the general call Gracie. Now, how do you get Gracie to do that dirty work for you?"

"I'll have my wife bribe her with flowers and chocolate and Christmas decorations."

"Excuse me?" Rick asked.

"Gracie loves to decorate for Christmas. My wife has access to a catalog of rare antique decorations. Gracie can be bribed, if you know how," he added.

Rick smiled. "An assistant district attorney working a bribe. What if somebody tells her boss?"

"He'll laugh," Ramirez assured him. "It's for a just cause, after all."

Rick started down to the jail in time to waylay the departing felon. He spoke to the probation officer on the way and arranged the conversation.

The man was willing to take a message to the general, for a price. That put them on the hot seat, because neither man could be seen offering illegal payment to a felon.

Then Rick had a brainstorm. "Wait a second." He'd spotted the janitor emptying trash baskets nearby. He took the man to one side, handed him two fifties and told him what to do.

The janitor, confused but willing to help, walked over to the prisoner and handed him the money. It was from him, he added, since the prisoner had been pleasant to him during his occupation in the jail. He wanted to help him get started again on the outside.

The prisoner, smiling, understood immediately what was going on. He took the money graciously, with a bow, and proceeded to sing the janitor's praises for his act of generosity. So the message was sent.

Gwen Cassaway was sitting at Rick's desk when he went back to his office, in the chair reserved for visitors. He hated the way his heart jumped at the sight of her. He fought down that unwanted feeling.

"Do they have to issue us these chairs?" she complained when he came in, closing the door behind him. "Honestly, only hospital waiting rooms have chairs that are more uncomfortable."

"The idea is to make you want to leave," he assured her. "What's up?" he added absently as he removed his holstered pistol from his belt and slid it into a desk drawer, then locked the drawer before he sat down. "Something about the case I assigned you to?"

She hesitated. This was going to be difficult. "Something else. Something personal."

He stared at her coolly. "I don't discuss personal issues with colleagues. We have a staff psychologist if you need counseling."

She let out an exasperated sigh. "Honestly, do

you have a steel rod glued to your spine?" she burst out. Then she realized what she'd said, clapped her hand over her mouth and looked horrified at the slip.

He didn't react. He just stared.

"I'm sorry!" she said, flustered. "I'm so sorry! I didn't mean to say that . . . !"

"Cassaway," he began.

"It's about the general," she blurted out.

His dark eyes narrowed. "Lately, everything is. Don't tell me. You're having an affair with him and you have to confess for the sake of your job."

She drew in a long breath. "Actually, the general *is* my job." She got up, opened her wallet and handed it to Rick.

He did an almost comical double take. He looked at her as if she'd grown leaves. "You're a fed?"

She nodded and grimaced. She took back the wallet after he'd looked at it again, just to make sure it didn't come from the toy department in some big store.

She put it back in her fanny pack. "Sorry I couldn't say something before, but they wouldn't let me," she said heavily as she sat down again, with her hands folded on her jeans.

"What the hell are you doing pretending to be a detective?" he asked with some exasperation.

"It was my boss's idea. I did start out with Atlanta P.D., but I've worked in counterterrorism for the agency for about four years now," she confessed. "I'm sorry," she repeated. "This wasn't my idea. They wanted me to find out how much you knew about your family history before they accidentally said or did something that would upset you."

He raised an eyebrow. "I've just been presented with a father who's an exiled South American dictator, whose existence I was unaware of. They didn't think that would upset me?"

"I asked Cash Grier to talk to your mother," she said. "You can't tell anybody. I was ordered not to talk to you about it. But they didn't say I couldn't ask somebody else to do it."

He was touched by her concern. Not that he liked her any better. "I wondered about your shooting skills," he said after a minute. "Not exactly something I expect in a run-of-the-mill detective."

She smiled. "I spend a lot of time on the gun range," she replied. "I've been champion of my unit for two years running."

"Our lieutenant was certainly surprised when he found himself outdone," he remarked.

"He's very nice."

He glared at her.

She wondered what he had against his superior officer, but she didn't comment. "I was told that a DEA officer is going to try to get someone to speak to General Machado about you."

"Yes. Gracie Pendleton will talk with him. Machado likes her."

"He kidnapped her!" she exclaimed. "And the man she's now married to!"

He nodded. "I know. He also saved her from being assaulted by one of Fuentes's men," he added.

"Oh. I didn't know that."

"She's fond of him, too," he replied. "Apparently, he makes friends even of his enemies. A couple of feds I know think he's one of the better insurgents," he added dryly.

"He did install democratic government in Barrera," she pointed out. "He instituted reforms that did away with unlawful detention and surveillance, he invited the foreign media in to oversee elections and he ousted half a dozen petty politicians who were robbing the poor and making themselves into feudal lords. From what we understand, one of those petty politicians helped Machado's second-in-command plan the coup that ousted him."

"While he was out of the country negotiating trade agreements," Rick agreed. "Stabbed in the back."

"Exactly. We'd love to have him back in power, but we can't actually do anything about it," she said quietly. "That's where you come in."

"The general doesn't even know me, let alone that I'm his biological son," he repeated. "Even if he did, I don't think he's going to jump up and invite me to baseball games."

"Soccer," she corrected. "He hates baseball."

His eyebrows lifted. "How do you know that?"

"I have a file on him," she said. "He likes strawberry ice cream, his favorite musical star is Marco Antonio Solís, he wears size 12 shoes and he plays classical guitar. Oh, he was an entertainer on a cruise ship in his youth."

"I did know about that. Not his shoe size," he added with twinkling dark eyes.

"He's never been romantically linked with any particular woman," she continued. "Although he was good friends with an American anthropologist who went to live in his country. She'd found an ancient site that was revolutionary and she was involved in a dig there. Apparently, there are some interesting ruins in Barrera."

"What happened to her?"

"Nobody knows. We couldn't even ascertain her name. What I was able to ferret out was only gossip."

He folded his hands on his desk. "So, you're a fed, I'm one detective short and you're supposed to be heading a murder investigation for me," he said curtly. "What do I do about that?"

"I've been working on it," she protested. "I'm making progress, too. As soon as we get the DNA profile back, I may be able to make an arrest in the college freshman's murder, and solve a cold case involving another dead coed. I have lots of information to go on, now, including eye-witness testimony that can place the suspect at the murdered woman's apartment just before she was killed."

He sat up. "Nice!"

"Thank you. I have an appointment to talk to her best friend, also, the one who took the photo that the suspect showed up in. She gave a statement to the crime scene detective that the victim had complained about visits from a man who made her uneasy."

"They'll let you continue to work on my case, even though you're a fed?"

"Until something happens in the general's case," she said. "I'm keeping up appearances."

"You slipped through the cracks," he translated.

She laughed. "Thanksgiving is just over the horizon and my boss gets a lot of business done in D.C. going from one party to another with his wife."

"I see."

"When is Mrs. Pendleton going to talk to the general, did the DEA agent say?"

He shook his head. "It's only a work in progress right now." He leaned back in his chair. "I thought my father was dead. My mother told me he was killed when I was just a baby. I didn't realize I had a father who never even knew I was on the way."

"He loves children," she pointed out.

"Yes, but I'm not a child."

"I noticed."

He glared at her.

She flushed and averted her eyes.

He felt guilty. "Sorry. I'm not dealing with this well."

"I can understand that," she replied. "I know it must be hard for you."

She had a nice voice, he thought. Soft and medium in pitch, and she colored it in pastels with emotion. He liked her voice. Her choice of T-shirts, however, left a lot to be desired. She had on one today that read Save a Turkey, Eat a Horse for Thanksgiving. He burst out laughing.

"Do you have an open line to a T-shirt manufacturer?" he asked.

"What? Oh!" She glanced down at her shirt. "Well, sort of. There's this online place that lets you make your own T-shirts. I do a lot of business with them, designing my own."

Now he understood her quirky wardrobe.

"Drives my boss nuts," she added with a grin. "He thinks I'm not dignified enough on the job."

"I'm sure you have casual days, even in D.C."

"I don't work in D.C.," she said. "I get sent wherever I'm needed. I live out of a suitcase mostly." She smiled wanly. "It's not much of a life. I loved it when I was younger, but I'd really love to have someplace permanent."

"You could get a job in a local office."

"I guess." She shrugged. "Meanwhile, I've got one right here. I'm sorry I didn't tell you who I was at first," she added. "I would have liked to be honest."

He sensed that. He grimaced. "It's hard for me, too, trying to understand the past. My mother, my adopted mother," he said, just to clarify the point, "said that the general was only fourteen when he fathered me. I'll be thirty-one this year, in late December. That would make him—" he stopped and thought "—forty-five." His eyebrows arched. "That's not a great age for a dictator."

She laughed. "He was forty-one when he became president of Barrera," she said. "In those four years, he did a world of good for his country. His adopted country."

"Yes, well, he's wanted in this country for kidnapping," he reminded her.

"Good luck trying to get him extradited," she cautioned. "First the Mexican authorities would have to actually apprehend him, and he's got a huge complex in northern Sonora. One report is that he even has a howitzer."

"True story," he said, leaning back in his chair. "Pancho Villa, who fought in the Mexican Revolution, was a folk hero in Mexico at the turn of the twentieth century. John Reed, a Harvard graduate and journalist, actually lived with him for several months."

"And wrote articles about his adventures there. They made them into a book," she said, shocking him. "I had to buy it from a rare book shop. It's one of my treasures."

CHAPTER 6

"I've read that book," Rick said with a slow smile. "*Insurgent Mexico*. I couldn't afford to buy it, unfortunately, so I got it on loan from the library. It was published in 1914. A rare book, indeed."

She shifted uncomfortably. She hadn't meant to let that bit slip. She was still keeping secrets from him. She shouldn't have been able to afford the book on her government salary. Her father had given it to her last Christmas. That was another secret she was keeping, too; her father's identity.

"And would you know Pancho Villa's real name?" he asked suddenly.

She grinned. "He was born Doroteo Arango," she said. The smile faded a little. "He changed his name to Pancho Villa, according to one source, because he was hunted by the authorities for killing a man who raped his younger sister. It put him on a path of lawlessness, but he fought all his life for a Mexico that was free of foreign oppression and a government that worked for the poor."

He smiled with pure delight. "You read Mexican history," he mused, still surprised.

"Well, yes, but the best of it is in Spanish, so I studied very hard to learn to read it," she confessed. She flushed. "I like the colonial histories, written by priests in the sixteenth century who sailed with the *conquistadores*."

"Spanish colonial history," he said.

She smiled. "I also like to read about Juan Belmonte and Manolete."

His eyebrows arched. "Bullfighters?" he exclaimed.

"Well, yes," she said. "Not the modern ones. I don't know anything about those. I found this book on Juan Belmonte, his biography. I was so fascinated by it that I started reading about Joselito and the others who fought bulls in Spain at the beginning of the twentieth century. They were so brave. Nothing but a cape and courage, facing a bull that was twice their size, all muscle and with horns so sharp . . ." She cleared her throat. "It's not PC to talk about it, I know."

"Yes, we mustn't mention blood sports," he joked. "The old bullfighters were like soldiers who fought in the world wars—tough and courageous. I like World War II history, particularly the North African theater of war."

Her eyes opened wide behind the lenses of her glasses. "Rommel. Patton. Montgomery. Alexander . . ."

His lips fell open. "Yes."

She laughed with some embarrassment. "I'm a history major," she said. "I took my degree in it." She didn't add that she came by her interest in military history quite naturally, nor that her grandfather had known General George S. Patton, Jr., personally.

"Well!"

"You have an associate's degree in criminal justice and you're going to night school working on your B.A.," she blurted out.

He laughed. "What's my shoe size?"

"Eleven." She cleared her throat. "Sorry. I have a file on you, too."

He leaned forward, his large dark eyes narrow. "I'll have to compile one on you. Just to be fair."

She didn't want him to do that, but she just nodded. Maybe he couldn't dig up too much, even if he tried. She kept her private life very private.

She stood up. "I need to get back to work. I just wanted to be honest with you, about my job," she said. "I didn't want you to think I was being deliberately deceitful."

He stood up, too. "I never thought that."

He walked with her to the door. "Uh, is the lieutenant still bringing you roses?" he asked, and could have slapped himself for even asking the question.

"Oh, certainly not," she said primly. "That was

just an apology, for using bad language in front of me."

"He's a widower," he said as they reached the door.

She paused and looked up at him. He was very close all of a sudden and she felt the heat from his body as her nostrils caught the faint, exotic scent of the cologne he used. He smelled very masculine and her heart went wild at the proximity. Her head barely topped his shoulder. He was tall and powerfully built, and she had an almost overwhelming hunger to lay her head on that shoulder and press close and bury her lips in that smooth, tanned throat.

She caught her breath and stepped back quickly. She looked up into his searching eyes and stood very still, like a cat in the sights of a hunter. She couldn't even think of anything to say.

Rick was feeling something similar. She smelled of wildflowers today. Her skin was almost translucent and he noticed that she wore little makeup. Her hair was caught up in a high ponytail, but he was certain that if she let it down, it would make a thick platinum curtain all the way to her waist. He wanted, badly, to loosen it and bury his mouth in it.

He stepped back, too. The feelings were uncomfortable. "Better get back to work," he said curtly. He was breathing heavily. His voice didn't sound natural.

"Yes. Uh, m-me, too," she stammered, and flushed, making her skin look even prettier.

He started to open the door for her. But he paused. "Someone told me that you like *The Firebird.*"

She laughed nervously. "Yes. Very much."

"The orchestra is doing a tribute to Stravinsky Friday night." He moved one shoulder. He shouldn't do this. But he couldn't help himself. "I have two tickets. I was going to take Mom, but she's going to have to cater some cattlemen's meeting in Jacobsville and she can't go." He took a breath. "So I was wondering . . ."

"Yes." She cleared her throat. "I mean, if you were going to ask me . . . ?" she blurted, embarrassed.

Her nervousness lessened his. He smiled at her in a way he never had, his chiseled mouth sensuous, his eyes very dark and soft. "Yes. I was going to ask you."

"Oh." She laughed, self-consciously.

He tipped her chin up with his bent forefinger and looked into her soft, pale green eyes. "Six o'clock? We'll have dinner first."

Her breath caught. Her heartbeat shook her T-shirt. "Yes," she whispered breathlessly.

His dark eyes were on her pretty bow of a mouth. It was slightly parted, showing her white teeth. He actually started bending toward it when his phone suddenly rang.

He jerked back, laughing deeply at his own helpless response to her. "Go to work," he said, but he grinned.

"Yes, sir." She started out the door. She looked back at him. "I live in the Oak Street apartments," she said. "Number 92."

He smiled back. "I'll remember."

She left, with obvious reluctance.

It took him a minute to realize that his phone was still ringing. He was going to date a colleague and the whole department would know. Well, what the hell, he muttered to himself. He was really tired of going to concerts and the ballet alone. She was a fed and she wouldn't be here long. Why shouldn't he have companionship?

Gwen got back to her own office and leaned back against the door with a long sigh. She was trembling from the encounter with Rick and so shocked at his invitation that she could barely get her breath back. He was going to date her. He wanted to take her out. She could barely believe it!

While she was savoring the invitation, her cell phone rang. She noted the number and opened it.

"Hi, Dad," she said, smiling. "How's it going?"

"Rough, or don't you watch the news, pudding?" he asked with a laugh in his deep voice as he used his nickname for her.

"I do," she said. "I'm really sorry. Politicians

124

should let the military handle military matters."

"Come up to D.C. and tell the POTUS that," he murmured.

"Why can't you just say President of the United States?" she teased.

"I'm in the military. We use abbreviations."

"I noticed."

"How's it going with you?"

"I'm working on a sensitive matter."

"I've been talking to your boss about it," he replied. "And I told him that I don't like having you put on the firing line like this."

She winced. She could imagine that encounter. Her boss, while very nice, was also as bullheaded as her father. It would have been interesting to see how it ended.

"And he told you . . . ?"

He sighed. "That I could mind my own damned business, basically," he explained. "We're a lot alike."

"I noticed."

"Anyway, I hope you're packing, and that the detective you're working with is, also."

"We both are, but the general isn't a bad man."

"He's wanted for kidnapping!"

"Yes, well, he's desperate for money, but he didn't really hurt anybody."

"A man was killed in his camp," he returned curtly.

"Yes, the general shot him for trying to assault

Gracie Pendleton," she replied. "He caught him in the act. Gracie was bruised and shaken, but he got to her just in time. The guy was one of the Fuentes organization."

There was a long silence. "I didn't hear that part."

"Not many people have."

He sighed. "Well, maybe he's not as bad a man as I thought he was."

"We want him on our side. He has a son that he didn't know about. We're trying to get an entrée into his camp, to make a contact with him. It isn't easy."

"I know about that, too." He paused. "How's your love life?" he teased.

She cleared her throat. "Actually, Sergeant Marquez just invited me to a symphony concert."

There was a longer pause. "He likes classical music?"

"Yes, and the ballet." Her eyes narrowed. "And no smart remarks, if you please."

"I like classical music."

"But you hate ballet," she pointed out. "And you think anybody who does is nuts."

"So I have a few interesting flaws," he conceded.

"He's also a military history buff," she added quickly. "World War II and North Africa."

"How ironic," he chuckled.

She smiled to herself. "Yes, isn't it?"

He drew in a long sigh. "You coming home for Christmas?"

"Of course," she agreed. She smiled sadly. "Especially this year."

"I'm glad." He bit off the words. "It hasn't been easy. Larry's wife calls me every other night, crying."

"Lindy will adjust," she said softly. "It's just going to take time. She and Larry were married for ten years and they didn't have children. That will make it harder for her. But she's strong. She'll manage."

"I hope so." There was a scraping sound, as if he was getting up out of a chair. "His commanding officer got drunk and wrecked a bar up in Maryland, while he was on R&R," he said.

"Larry's death wasn't his fault," she replied tersely. "Any officer who goes into a covert situation knows the risks and has to be willing to take them."

"I told him that," her father replied. "Damn it, he cried . . . !" He cleared his throat, choking back the emotion. "I called up Brigadier Langston and told him to get that man some help before he becomes a statistic. He promised he would."

"General Langston was fond of Larry, too," she said quietly. "I remember him at the funeral . . ."

There was a pause. "Let's talk about something else."

127

"Okay. How do you feel about giving chickens the vote?"

He burst out laughing.

"Or we could decide where we're going to eat on Christmas Eve, because I'm not spending my days off in the kitchen," she said.

"Good thing. We'd starve or die of carbon monoxide poisoning," he replied.

"I can cook! I just don't like to."

"If you'd use timers, we'd have food that didn't turn black before we got to eat it," he said. "I can cook anything," he added smugly.

"I remember." She sighed. "Rick's mom is a great cook," she replied. "She owns a restaurant."

"She does? You should marry him. You'd never have to worry about cooking again." He chuckled.

She blushed. "It's just a date, Dad."

"Your first one in how many years . . . ?"

"Stop that," she muttered. "I date."

"You went to the Laundromat with a guy who lived in your apartment building," he burst out. "That's not a date!"

"It was fun. We ate potato chips and discussed movies while our clothes got done," she replied.

He shook his head. "Pudding, you're hopeless."

"Thanks!"

"I give up. I have to go. I've got a meeting with the Joint Chiefs in ten minutes."

"More war talk?"

"More withdrawal talk," he said. "There's a

rumor that the POTUS is going to offer me Hart's job."

"You're kidding!"

"That's what they're saying."

"Will you take it?" she asked, excited.

"Watch the news and we'll find out."

"That would be great!"

"I might be in a position to do something more useful," he said. "But, we'll see. I guess I'd do it, if they ask me."

"Good for you!"

"Say, do you ever see Grange?"

"Grange? You mean, the Pendletons' foreman?" she asked, disconcerted.

"Yes. Winslow Grange. He was in my last overseas command." He smiled. "Had a real pig of an officer, who sent him into harm's way understrength and with a battle plan that some kindergarten kid could have come up with. Grange tied him up, put him in the trunk of his own car and led the assault himself. He was invited to leave the army with an honorable discharge or be court-martialed. He left. But he came back to testify against his commanding officer, who was dishonorably discharged after a nasty trial."

"Good enough for him," she said curtly.

"I do agree. Anyway, Winslow is a friend of mine. I'd love to see him sometime. You might pass that along. We could always use someone like him in D.C. if he gets tired of horse poop."

She wondered if she should tell her father what his buddy Grange was rumored to be doing right now, but that was probably a secret she should keep. "If I see him, I'll tell him," she promised.

"Take care of yourself, okay? You're the only family I've got left." His deep voice was thick with emotion.

"Same here," she replied. "Love you, Dad."

"Mmm-hmm." He wasn't going to say it out loud. He never did. But he loved her, so she didn't make a smart remark.

"I'll call you in a few days, just to check in. Okay?"

"That's a deal." His hand went over the receiver. "Yes, I'm on my way," he told someone else. "Gotta go. See you, kid."

"Bye, Dad."

He hung up. She put the phone back in her pocket. It seemed to be a day for revelations.

She had a beautiful little couture black dress, with expensive black slingbacks and a frilly black shawl that she'd gotten in Madrid. She wore those for her date with Rick, and she let her hair down, brushing it until it was shiny, like a pale satin curtain down her back. She left her glasses off for once. If she wasn't driving, she didn't need them, and a symphony concert didn't really require perfect vision.

Rick wore a dinner jacket and a black tie. His own hair was still in its elegant ponytail, but tied with a neat black ribbon. He looked very sharp.

He stared at her with disconcerting interest when she opened the door, taking in the nice fit of her dress with its modest rounded neckline and lacy hem that hit just at mid-calf. Her pretty little feet were in strappy high heels that left just a hint of the space between her toes visible. It was oddly sexy.

"You look . . . very nice," he said, his eyes taking in her flushed, lovely complexion and her perfect mouth, just dabbed with pale lipstick.

"Thanks! So do you," she replied, laughing nervously.

He produced a box from behind his back and handed it to her. It was a beautiful cymbidium orchid, much like the ones she had back at her father's home that the housekeeper faithfully misted each day.

"It's lovely!" she exclaimed.

He raised one shoulder and smiled self-consciously. "They wanted to give me one you wore around the wrist, but I explained that we weren't going to a dance and I wanted one that pinned."

"I like this kind best." She took it out of the box and pinned it to the dress, smiling at the way it complemented the dark background. "Thanks."

"My pleasure. Shall we go?"

"Yes!"

She grabbed her evening bag, closed the door and locked it and let him help her into his pickup truck.

"I should have something more elegant to drive than this," he muttered as he climbed in beside her.

"But I love trucks!" she exclaimed. "My dad has one that he drives around our place when he's home."

He grinned. "Well, maybe I'll get a nice car one day."

"It doesn't matter what you go in, as long as it gets you to your destination," she pointed out. "I even like Humvees."

His eyebrows arched. "And where do you get to ride in those?"

She bit her tongue. "Uh . . ."

"I forgot. Your brother was in the military, you said," he interrupted. "Sorry. I didn't mean to bring back sad memories for you."

She drew in a long breath. "He died doing what he felt was important for his country," she replied. "He was very patriotic and spec ops was his life."

His eyebrows arched.

"He died in a classified operation," she added. "His commanding officer just went on a huge bender. He feels responsible. He ordered the incursion."

His eyes softened. "That's the sort of man I wouldn't mind serving under," he said quietly. "A man with a conscience, who cares about his men."

She smiled. "My dad's like that, too. I mean, he's a man with a conscience," she said quickly.

He didn't notice the slip. He reached out and touched her soft cheek. "I'm sorry for your loss," he said. "I don't have siblings. But I wish I did."

She managed a smile. "Larry was a wonderful brother and a terrific husband. His wife is taking it hard. They didn't have any kids."

"Tough."

She nodded. "It's going to be hard to get through Christmas," she said. "Larry was a nut about it. He came home to Lindy every year and he brought all sorts of foreign decorations with him. We've got plenty that he sent us . . ."

He moved closer. His big hands framed her face and lifted it. Her pale green eyes were swimming in tears. He bent, helpless, and softly kissed away the tears.

"Life is often painful," he whispered. "But there are compensations."

While he spoke, his chiseled lips were moving against her eyelids, her nose, her cheeks. Finally, as she held her breath in wild anticipation, his lips hovered just over her perfect bow of a mouth. She could feel his breath, taste its minty freshness, see the hard curve of his lips that filled her vision to the extent of anything else.

She hung there, at his mouth, her eyes half closed, her skin tingling from the warm strength of his hands framing her face, waiting, waiting, waiting . . . !

He drew in an unsteady breath and bent closer, logic flying out the window as the wildflower scent of her made him weak. Her mouth was perfect. He wanted to feel its softness under his lips, taste her. He was sure that she was going to be delicious . . .

The sudden sound of a horn blowing raucously on the street behind them shocked them apart. He blinked, as if he was under the influence of alcohol. She didn't seem much calmer. She fumbled with her purse.

"I guess we should go," he said with a forced laugh. "We want to have enough time to eat before the concert."

"Y . . . yes," she agreed.

"Seat belt," he added, nodding toward it.

"Oh. Yes! I usually put it on at once," she added as she fumbled it into place.

He laughed, securing his own.

Her shy smile made him feel taller. Involuntarily, his fingers linked with hers as he started the truck and pulled out into traffic. He wouldn't even let himself think about how he'd gone in headfirst with a colleague, against all his best instincts. He was too happy.

They ate at a nice restaurant in San Antonio, one with a flamenco theme and a live guitarist with a Spanish dancer in a beautiful red dress with puffy sleeves and the ruffled, long-trained dress that was familiar to followers of the dance style. The performance was short, but the applause went on for a long time. The duet was impressive.

"What a treat," she said enthusiastically. "They're so good!"

"Yes, they are." He grinned. "I love flamenco."

"So do I. I bought this old movie, *Around the World in 80 Days*, and it had a guy named Jose Greco and his flamenco dance troupe in it. That's when I fell in love with flamenco. He was so talented," she said.

"I've seen tapes of Jose Greco dancing," he replied. "He truly was phenomenal."

"My mother used to love Latin dances," she said dreamily, smiling. "She could do them all."

"Is she still alive?" he asked carefully.

She hesitated. She shook her head. "We lost her when I was in my final year of high school. Dad was overseas and couldn't even come back for the funeral, so Larry and I had to do everything. Dad never got over it. He was just starting to, when Larry died."

"Why couldn't your father come home?" he asked, curious.

She swallowed. "He was involved in a classified mission," she said. She held up a hand when he started to follow up with another question, smiling to lessen the sting. "Sorry, but he couldn't even tell me what he was doing. National security stuff."

His eyebrows arched. "Your dad's in the military?"

She hesitated. But it wouldn't hurt to agree. He was. But Rick would be thinking of a regular soldier, and her dad was far from regular. "Yes," she replied.

"I see."

"You don't, but I can't say any more," she told him.

"I guess not. Wouldn't want to tick off the brass by saying something out of turn, right?" he teased.

"Right." She had to fight a laugh. Her father was the brass; one of the highest ranking officers in the U.S. Army, in fact.

The waiter who took their order was back quickly with cups of hot coffee and the appetizers, buffalo wings and French fries with cheese and chili dip.

Rick tasted the wings and laughed as he put it quickly back down. "Hot!" he exclaimed.

"I'm glad I'm wearing black," she sighed. "If I had on a white dress, it would be red-and-white polka dotted when I finished eating. I wear most of my food."

His dark eyebrows arched and he grinned. "Me, too."

She laughed. "I'm glad it's not just me."

He tried again with the French fries. "These are really good. Here. Taste."

She let him place it at her lips. She bit off the end and sighed. "Delicious!"

"They have wonderful food, including a really special barbecue sauce for the wings. Want to know where they got it?" he asked mischievously.

"From your mother?" she guessed.

He shook his head. "It seems that FBI senior agent Jon Blackhawk came here to eat with his brother, Kilraven, one night. Jon tasted their barbecue sauce, made a face, got up, walked into the kitchen and proceeded to have words with the chef."

"You're kidding!"

"I'm not. It didn't come to blows, but only because Jon put on an apron and showed the chef how to make a proper barbecue sauce. When the chef tasted it, so the story goes, he asked which cordon bleu academy in Paris Mr. Blackhawk had attended. He got the shock of his life when Jon named it." He grinned. "You see, he actually went to Paris and took courses. His new wife is one lucky woman. She'll never have to go in the kitchen unless she really wants to."

"I heard about them," she replied. "That's one interesting family."

He munched a French fry thoughtfully. "I'd love to have kids," he said solemnly. "A big family to make up for what I never had." His expression was bitter. "Barbara is the best mother on the planet, but I wish I'd had brothers and sisters."

"You do at least still have a father living," she pointed out.

"A father who's going to get the shock of his life when he's introduced to his grown-up son," he said. "And I wonder if Ramirez has had any luck getting his sister-in-law to approach the general."

As if in answer to the question, his cell phone began vibrating. He checked the number, gave her a stunned glance and got to his feet. "I'll be right back. I have to take this."

She nodded. She liked his consideration for the other diners. He took the call outside on the street, so that he wouldn't disturb other people with his conversation.

He was back in less than five minutes. He sat back down. "Imagine that," he said on a hollow laugh. "Gracie talked to the general. He wants us to come to the border Monday morning for a little chat, as he put it."

Her eyebrows arched. "Progress," she said, approving.

He sighed. "Yes. Progress." He didn't add that he had misgivings and he was nervous as hell. He just finished eating.

CHAPTER 7

Rick was preoccupied through the rest of the meal. Gwen didn't talk much, either. She knew he had to be unsettled about the trip to the border, for a lot of reasons.

He held her hand on the way to the car, his strong fingers tangling in hers.

"It will be all right," she blurted out.

They reached the passenger door and he paused, looking down at her. "Will it?"

"You're a good man," she said. "He'll be very proud of you."

He was uncertain. "You think?"

She loved the smell of his body, the warm strength of it near her. She loved everything about him. "Yes."

He smiled tenderly. She made him feel tall, powerful, important. Women had made him feel undervalued for years, mostly by thinking of him as nothing more than a friend. Gwen was different. She was a working girl, from his own middle-class strata. She was pretty, in her way, and smart. And she knew her way around a handgun, he thought amusedly. But she also stirred his senses in a new and exciting way.

"You're nice," he said suddenly.

She grimaced. "Rub it in."

"No. Nice, in a very positive way," he replied. His expression was somber. "I don't like sophisticated women. I like brains in a woman, and even athletic outlooks. But I do mind women who think of themselves as party favors. You get me?"

She smiled. "I feel the same way about men like that."

He smiled. "You and I, we don't belong in a modern setting."

"We'd look very nice in a Victorian village," she agreed. "Like Edward in the *Twilight* vampire series of books and movies. I love those. I guess I've seen the movies ten times each and read the books on my iPod every night."

"I don't watch vampire movies. I like werewolves."

"Oh, but there are werewolves in them, too. Nice werewolves."

"You're kidding."

She hesitated. "I've got all the DVDs. I was wondering . . ."

He moved a step closer, so that she was backed into the car door. "You were wondering?"

"Uh, yes, if you'd like to maybe watch the movies with me?" she asked him. "I could make a pizza. Or we could . . . order . . . one . . . ?"

She was whispering now, and her voice was breaking because his mouth had moved closer with every whispered word until it was right against her soft lips.

"Gwen?"

"Hmm?"

"Shut up," he whispered against her lips, and his crushed down on them with warm, sensual, insistent hunger.

A muffled sob broke from her throat as she lifted her arms and pressed her body as close as she could get it to his tall, powerful form. He groaned, too, as the insane delight pulsed through him like fire.

He moved, shifting her, so that one long leg was between her skirt, and his mouth was suddenly invasive, starving.

"Detective!"

He heard a voice. It sounded close. And shocked. And angry. He lifted his head, still reeling from Gwen's soft mouth.

"Hmm?" he murmured, turning his head.

"Detective Sergeant Marquez," a deep, angry voice repeated.

"Sir!" He jumped back, almost saluted, and tried to look normal. He hoped his jacket was covering a blatant reminder of his body's interest in Gwen's.

"What the hell are you doing?" Lieutenant Hollister asked gruffly.

"It's okay, sir," Gwen faltered. "He was, uh, helping me get my earring unstuck from my dress."

He blinked and scowled. "What?"

"My earring, sir." She dangled it in her hand. "It caught on my dress. Detective Marquez was helping me get it loose. I guess it did look odd, the position we were in." She laughed with remarkable acting ability.

"Oh. I see." Hollister cleared his throat. He shoved his hands in his pockets. "I'm very sorry. It looked, well, I mean . . ." He cleared his throat again. He scowled. "I thought you didn't date colleagues," he shot at Marquez, who had by reciting multiplication tables made a remarkably quick recovery.

"I don't, sir," Marquez agreed. "We both like flamenco, and there's a dancer here . . ."

Hollister held up his hand and declared, "Say no more. That's why I came. Alone, sadly," he added with a speculative and rather sad look at Gwen.

"She's a great dancer," Gwen said. "And that guitarist!"

He nodded. "Her husband."

"Really!" Gwen exclaimed.

"Oh, yes. They've appeared all over Europe. I understand they're being considered for a bit part in a movie that's filming near here next year."

"That would be so lovely for them," Gwen enthused.

Rick checked his watch. "We'd better go. I've got an appointment early Monday morning. I thought I'd brush up on my Spanish over the weekend," he added dryly.

"Yes, I heard about that," Hollister said quietly. "It will go all right," he told Rick. "You'll see."

Rick was touched. "Thanks."

Hollister shrugged. "You're a credit to my department. Don't let him talk you into going to South America, okay?"

Rick smiled. "I'm not much good with rocket launchers."

"Me, neither," the lieutenant agreed. He glanced at Gwen and smiled. "Well, sorry about the mistake. Have a good evening."

"You, too, sir," Gwen said, and Rick nodded assent.

Hollister nodded back and walked, distracted, toward the restaurant.

Rick helped Gwen into the truck and burst out laughing. So did she.

"Did I ever tell you that I minored in theater in college?" she asked. "They said I had promise."

"You could make movies," he said flatly. He shook his head as he started the truck. "Quick thinking."

"Thanks." She flushed a little.

Neither of them mentioned that they'd been so far gone that anything could have happened, right there in the parking lot, if the lieutenant hadn't shown up. But it was true. Also true was the look the lieutenant had been giving them. He seemed to have more than the usual interest in Gwen. He wasn't really the sort of man to put a rose on a woman's desk unless he meant it. Rick was thinking that he had some major competition there, if he didn't watch his step. Hollister's tone hadn't been one of outraged decorum so much as jealous anger.

Rick left Gwen at her door. He was more cautious this time, but he did pull her close and kiss her good-night with barely restrained passion.

She held him, kissing him back, loving the warm, soft press of his mouth on hers.

"I'm out of practice," he murmured as he stepped back.

"Me, too," she said breathlessly, her eyes full of stars as they met his in the light from the security lamps.

"I guess we could practice with each other," he murmured dryly.

She flushed and laughed nervously. "I'd like that."

"Yes. So would I." He bent again, brushing his mouth lightly over hers and forcing himself not to go in headfirst. "Are you coming along, in the morning?"

She nodded. "I have to."

He smiled. "Good. I could use the moral support."

She smiled back. "Thanks."

"Well. I'll see you at the office Monday."

"Yes."

He turned and took a step. He stopped. He turned. She was still standing there, her expression confused, waiting, still . . .

He walked back to her. "Unlock the door," he said quietly.

She fumbled the key into the lock and opened it. He closed it behind him, his arms enveloping her in the dark hallway, illuminated by a single small lamp in the living room. His mouth searched for hers, found it, claimed it, possessed it hungrily.

His arms were insistent, locking her against the length of his powerful body. She moaned, a sound almost like a sob of pleasure.

He was feeling something very similar.

"What the hell," he whispered into her lips as he bent and lifted her, still kissing her, and carried her to the long, soft sofa.

They slid down onto it together, his body covering hers, one long leg insinuating itself between her skirt, between her soft thighs. His lean hands went to the back of the dress, finding the hook and the zipper.

She didn't even have the presence of mind to protest. She was drowning in pleasure. She'd never felt anything remotely similar to the sensations that were washing over her like ripples of unbelievable delight.

He slid the dress off her arms, along with the tiny straps of the black slip she wore under it, exposing a small, black-lace bra that revealed more than it covered. She had pretty little breasts, firm and very soft.

His hand slid under the bra, savoring the warm softness of the flesh, exciting the hard little tip, making her shiver with new sensations.

She hadn't done this before. He knew it without being told. He smiled against her mouth. It was exciting, and new, to be the first man. He never had been. Not that there had even been that many women that he'd been almost intimate with. And, in recent years, nobody. Like Gwen, he'd never indulged in casual sex. He was as innocent, in his way, as she was. Well, he knew a little more than she did. When he touched his mouth to her breast, she lifted toward his lips with a shocked little gasp. He smiled as his mouth opened, taking the hard tip inside and pulling at it gently with his tongue.

Her nails bit into the muscles of his arms as he removed his jacket and tie and shirt, wanting so badly to be closer, closer . . .

She felt air on her skin and then the hard, warm press of hair and muscle as they locked together, both bare from the waist up.

His mouth was insistent now, hungry, demanding. She felt his hand sliding up her bare thigh and she knew that very soon they would reach a point from which there was no return.

"N . . . no," she whispered, pushing at his chest. "Rick? Rick!"

He heard her voice through a bloodred haze of desire that locked his muscles so tightly that he could barely move for the tension. She was saying something. What? It sounded like . . . no?

He lifted his head. He looked into wide, uneasy green eyes. He felt her body tensed, shivering.

"I'm sorry . . ." she began.

He blinked once, twice. He drew in a breath that sounded as ragged as he felt. "Good Lord," he exhaled.

She swallowed. They were very intimate. Neither of them had anything on above the waist. His hand was still on her thigh. He removed it quickly and lifted up just a little, his high cheekbones flushing when he got a sudden, stark, uninterrupted view of her pretty pink breasts with tight little dusky pink tips very urgently stating the desire of the owner for much more than looking.

Embarrassed, she drew her hands up over them as he levered himself away and sat up.

"I'm sorry," he said, averting his eyes while she fumbled her dress back on. "I didn't mean to . . ."

"Of c-course not," she stammered. "Neither did I. It's all right."

He laughed. His body felt as if it had been hit

with a bat several times in strategic places and he ached from head to toe. "Sure it is."

"Oh, I'm sorry!" she groaned. She wasn't experienced, but she had friends who were, and she knew what was wrong with him. "Here, just a sec."

She went to the kitchen and came back with a cold beer from the fridge. "Detective Rogers comes over from time to time and she likes this brand of light beer," she explained. "I don't drink, but I think people need to sometimes. You need to, a little . . . ?"

He gave her an exasperated sigh. "Gwen, I'm a police detective sergeant!"

"Yes, I know . . ."

"I can't take a drink and drive!"

She stared at him, looked at the beer. "Oh."

He burst out laughing. It broke the ice and slowly he began to feel normal again.

She looked around them. His jacket and shirt and tie, and her shoes and his holster and pistol were lying in a heap beside the sofa.

His gaze followed hers. He laughed again. "Well."

"Yes. Uh. Well." She looked at the can of beer, laughed, and set it down. Her glasses were where she'd tossed them on the end table but she didn't put them on. She didn't want to see his expression. She was already embarrassed.

He put his shirt and tie back on and slipped into

his jacket before he replaced the holstered pistol on his belt. "At least you don't object to the gun," he mused.

She shrugged. "I usually have a concealed carry in my purse," she confessed.

His eyebrows arched. "No ankle holster?" he asked.

She made a face. "Weighs down my leg too much."

He nodded. He looked at her in a different way now. Possessively. Hungrily. He moved forward, but he only took her oval face in his hands and searched her eyes, very close up. He was somber.

"From now on," he said gently, "we say goodnight at the door. Right?"

He was hinting at a relationship. "From now on?" she said hesitantly.

He nodded. He searched her eyes. "There aren't that many women running around loose who belong to the Victorian era, don't mind firearms and like to watch flamenco dancing."

She smiled with pure delight. "I was going to say the same about you—well, you're not a woman, of course."

"Of course."

He bent and kissed her very softly. He lifted his head and his large brown eyes narrowed. "If Hollister puts another rose on your desk, I'm going to deck him, and I don't care if he fires me."

Her face became radiant. "Really?"

"Really." His jaw tautened. "You're mine."

She flushed. She lowered her eyes to his strong neck, where a pulse beat very strongly. She nodded.

He hugged her close, rocked her in his arms. He drew in a long breath, finally, and let her go. He smiled ruefully. "After we get through talking with the general, Monday, I'm going to take you to meet my mother."

"You are?"

"You'll love her. She'll love you, too," he promised. He glanced at his watch and grimaced. "I have to get going. I'll pick you up here at 6:00 a.m. sharp, okay?"

"I could drive to the office . . ."

"I'll pick you up here."

She smiled. Her eyes were bright with pleasure. "Okay."

He chuckled. "Lock the door after me."

"I will. I really enjoyed the flamenco."

"So did I. I know another Latin dance club over on the west side of town. We'll go there next time. Do you like Mexican food?"

"Love it."

He smiled. "Theirs is pretty hot."

"No worries, I don't have any taste buds left. I eat jalapenos raw," she added with a grin.

"Whew! My kind of girl."

She grinned. "I noticed."

He laughed, kissed her hair and walked out the door.

After he climbed back into the pickup truck, he paused and waited until she was safely in her apartment before he drove off.

She didn't sleep that night. Not a wink. She was too excited, exhilarated and hungrily, passionately really in love for the first time in her life.

Rick was somber and nervous Monday morning when he picked Gwen up for the drive to the border. It had turned cold again and she was wearing a sweater and thick jeans with a jacket and boots.

"Summer yesterday, winter today," she remarked, readjusting her seat belt.

"That's Texas," he said fondly.

"Is Ramirez going to meet us at the border station?"

"Yes," he said. "He and Gracie."

Her eyebrows arched. "Mrs. Pendleton is coming, too? Isn't that dangerous?"

"We're not going over the border," he reminded her. "Just up to it."

"Oh. Okay."

He glanced at her, warm memories of the night before still in his dark eyes. She was lovely, he thought. Pretty and smart and good with a gun.

She felt his eyes but she didn't meet them. She was nervous, too. She worried about how he might feel when he learned the truth about her own background. She was still keeping secrets. She hoped he wouldn't feel differently when he learned them.

But right now, the biggest secret of all was about to be revealed to a man who had no apparent family and seemed to be content with his situation. Gwen wondered how the general would feel when he was introduced to a son he didn't even know existed.

They pulled up to the small border station, which wasn't much more than an adobe building beside the road, next to a cross arm that was denoted as the Mexican-American border, with appropriate warning signs.

A tall, sandy-haired man came out to meet them. He introduced himself as the border patrol agent in charge, Don Billings, and indicated a Lincoln town car sitting just a little distance way. He motioned.

The car pulled up, stopped and Rodrigo Ramirez got out, going around to open the door for his sister-in-law, Gracie Pendleton. They came forward and introductions were made.

Gracie was blonde and pretty and very pregnant. She laughed. "The general is going to be surprised when he sees me," she said with a grin. "I didn't mention my interesting condition. Jason and I are just over the moon!"

"Is it a boy or a girl?" Gwen wanted to know.

"We didn't let them tell us," she said. "We

want it to be a surprise, so I bought everything yellow instead of pink or blue."

Gwen laughed. "I'd like it to be a surprise, too, if I ever had a baby." Her eyes were dreamy. "I'd love to have a big family."

Rick was watching her and his heart was pounding. He'd like a big family, too. Her family. He cleared his throat. Memories of last night were causing him some difficulty in intimate places. He thought of sports until he calmed down a little.

"He should be here very soon," Ramirez said.

Even as he spoke, a pickup truck came along the dusty road from across the border, stopped and was waved through by the border agent.

The truck stopped. Two doors opened. Winslow Grange, wearing one of the very new high-tech camouflage patterned suits with an automatic pistol strapped to his hip, came forward. Right beside him was a tall, elegant-looking Hispanic man with thick, wavy black hair and large black eyes in a square face with chiseled lips and a big grin for Gracie.

"A baby?" he enthused. "How wonderful!"

She laughed, taking his outstretched hands. "Jason and I think so, too. How have you been?"

"Very busy," he said, indicating Grange. "We're planning a surprise party." He wiggled his eyebrows at the border agent. "I'm sorry that I can't say more."

"So am I." The border patrolman chuckled.

Gwen came forward, her eyes curious and welcoming at the same time. "You and I haven't met, but I think you've heard of me," she said gently. She held out her hand. "I'm Gwendolyn Cassaway. CIA."

He shook her hand warmly, and then raised it to his lips. He glanced at the man with her, a tall young man with long black hair in a pony-tail and an oddly familiar face. "Your boy-friend?" he asked, lifting an eyebrow at the reaction the young man gave when he kissed Gwen's hand.

"Uh, well, uh, I mean . . ." She cleared her throat. "This is Detective Sergeant Ricardo Marquez, San Antonio Police Department."

General Emilio Machado looked at the younger man with narrowed, intent eyes. "Marquez."

"Yes."

Machado was curious. "You look familiar, somehow. Do I know you?"

He studied the general quietly. "No. But my birth mother was Dolores Ortíz. She was from Sonora. I look like her."

Machado stared at him intently. "She lived in Sonora, in a little village called Dolito. I knew her once," he said. "She married a man named Jackson," he added coldly.

"My stepfather," Rick said curtly.

"I have heard about your late stepfather. He was a brutal man."

Rick liked Machado already. "Yes. I have the scars to prove it," he added quietly.

Machado drew in a long breath. He looked around him. "This is a very unusual place to meet with federal agents, and I feel that I am being set up."

"Not at all," Gwen replied. "But we do have something to tell you. Something that might be upsetting."

Nobody spoke. There were somber, grim faces all around.

"You brought a firing squad?" Machado mused, looking from one to the other. "Or you lured me here to arrest me for kidnapping Gracie?"

"None of the above," Gwen said quietly. She took a deep breath. This was a very unpleasant chore she'd been given. "We were doing a routine background check on you for our files and we came across your relationship with Dolores Ortíz. She gave birth to a child out of wedlock down in Sonora. Thirty-one years ago."

Machado was doing quick math in his head. He looked at Rick pointedly, with slowly growing comprehension. The man had looked familiar. Was it possible . . . ? He moved a step closer and cocked his head as he studied the somber-faced young man.

Then he laughed coldly. "Ah. Now I see. You know that I have spies in my country who are even now planting the seeds of revolution. You

155

know that I have an army and that I am almost certain to retake the government of Barrera. So you are searching for ways to ingratiate yourself with me . . . excuse me, with my oil and natural gas reserves as well as my very strategic location in South America." He gave Rick a hard glance. "You produce a candidate for my son, and think that I will accept your word that he is who he says he is."

"I haven't said a damned thing," Rick snapped back icily.

Machado's eyebrows shot up. "You deny their conclusion?"

Rick glared at him. "You think I'm thrilled to be lined up as the illegitimate son of some exiled South American dictator?"

Machado just stared at him for a minute. Then he burst out laughing.

"Rick," Gwen groaned from beside him.

"I was perfectly content to think my real father was in a grave somewhere in Mexico," Rick continued. "And then she showed up with this story . . ." He pointed at Gwen.

She raised her hand. "Cash Grier told your mother," she reminded him quickly. "I had nothing to do with telling you."

' "All right, my mother told me," he continued.

"Your mother is dead," Machado said, frowning.

"Barbara Ferguson, in Jacobsville, adopted

156

me when my mother and stepfather were killed in an auto accident," Rick continued. "She runs the café there."

Machado didn't speak. He'd never considered the possibility that Dolores would become pregnant. They'd been very close until her parents discovered them one night in an outbuilding and her father threatened to kill Machado if he ever saw him again. He'd gone to work for a big land-owner soon afterward and moved to another village. He hadn't seen Dolores again.

Could she have been pregnant? They'd done nothing to prevent a child. But he'd only been fourteen. He couldn't have fathered a son at that age, surely? In fact, he'd never fathered another child in the years since, and he had been coaxed into trying, at least once. The attempt had ended in total failure. It had hurt his pride, hurt his ego, made him uncertain about his manhood. He had thought, since then, that he must be sterile.

But here was, if he could believe the statement, proof of his virility. Could this really be his son?

He moved forward a step. Yes, the man had his eyes. He had Dolores's perfect teeth, as well. He was tall and powerfully built, as Machado was. His hair was long and black and straight, without the natural waves that were in Machado's. But, then, Dolores had long black hair that was smooth as silk and thick and straight.

"You think I would take your word for something this important, even with Gracie's help?" he asked Rick.

"Hey, I didn't come here to convince you of anything," Rick said defensively. "She—" he indicated Gwen "—got him—" he nodded at Ramirez "—to call her—" he pointed toward Gracie "—to have you meet us here. I got pulled into it because some feds think you'll listen to me even if you won't listen to them." He shrugged. "Of course, they haven't decided what to have me tell you just yet. I presume that's in the works and they'll let me know when they can agree on what day it is."

Machado listened to him, pursed his lips and laughed. "Sounds exactly like government policy to me. And I should know. I was head of a government once." His eyes narrowed and glittered. "And I will be, once again."

"I believe you," Gwen agreed.

"But for now," Machado continued, studying Rick. "What evidence exists that you really are my son? And it had better be good."

CHAPTER 8

"Don't look at me," Rick said quietly. "I didn't come here to prove anything."

Gwen moved forward, removing a paper from her purse. "We were sure that you wouldn't accept anyone's word, General," she said gently. "So we took the liberty of having a DNA profile made from Sergeant Marquez's last physical when blood was drawn." She gave Rick an apologetic glance. "Sorry."

Rick sighed. "Accepted."

The general read the papers, frowned, read some more and finally handed them back. "That's pretty convincing."

Gwen nodded.

He glanced at Rick, who was standing apart from the others, hard-faced, with his hands deep in the pockets of his slacks.

The general studied him from under thick black eyelashes, with some consternation. His whole life had just been turned upside-down. He had a son. The man was a law enforcement officer. He was not bad-looking, seemed intelligent, too. Of course, there was that severe attitude problem . . .

"I don't like baseball," Rick said curtly when he noticed how the general was eyeing him.

Machado's thick eyebrows levered up. "You don't like baseball . . . ?"

"In case you were thinking of father-son activities," Rick remarked drolly. "I don't like baseball. I like soccer."

Machado's dark eyes twinkled. "So do I."

"See?" Gwen said, grasping at straws, because this was becoming awkward. "Already, something in common . . ."

"Get down!"

While she was trying to understand the quick command from the general, Rick responded by tackling her. Rodrigo had Gracie in the limo, which had bulletproof glass, and Machado hit the ground with his pistol drawn at the same time Grange opened up with an army-issue repeating rifle.

"What the hell . . . !" Rick exclaimed as he leveled his own automatic, along with Gwen, at an unseen adversary, tracking his direction from the bullets hitting the dust a few yards away.

"Carver, IED, now!" Grange called into a walkie-talkie.

Seconds later, there was a huge explosion, a muffled cry, and a minute later, the sound of an engine starting and roaring, a dust cloud becoming visible as a person or persons unknown took off in the distance.

Grange grinned. "I always have a backup plan," he remarked.

"Good thing," Gwen exclaimed. "I didn't even consider an ambush!"

"Your father would have," Grange began.

She held up her hand and gave a curt shake of her head.

"You know her father?" Rick asked curiously.

"We were poker buddies, a few years back," Grange said. "Good man."

"Thanks," Gwen said, and she wasn't referring totally to the compliment. Grange would keep her secret; she saw it in his eyes.

Rick was brushing thick dust off his jacket and slacks. "Damn. They just came back from the dry cleaner."

"You should wear cotton. It cleans better," Machado suggested, indicating his own jeans and cotton shirt.

"Who was that, do you think?" Gwen asked somberly.

"Fuentes." Machado spat. "He and I have parted company. He amuses himself by sniping at me and my men."

"The drug lord? I thought his family was dead!" Gwen exclaimed.

"Most of it is. This is the last one of the Fuentes brothers, the stupid one, and he's clinging to power by his fingernails," the general told her. "He spies on me for a federal agency. Not yours," he told Gwen with a smile.

Ramirez left Gracie in the car and came back. "I don't think she should risk coming out here in the open," he said.

"I agree. She is all right?" Machado asked with some concern.

"Yes. Gracie really has guts," he replied. He frowned. "Which agency is Fuentes spying for?"

"Yours, I think, my friend," Machado told the DEA agent.

Ramirez let out a sigh. "We know there's a mole in our agency, someone very high level. We've never found out who it is."

"You should set Kilraven on him," Gwen mused dryly.

"I probably should," Ramirez agreed. "But we have our hands full right now with Mexican military coming over the border to protect drug shipments." He glanced toward the border patrol agent, who was talking to Gracie through a cracked window. "Our men on the border are in peril, always. We almost lost one some months ago, an agent named Kirk. He was very nearly killed. He left the agency and went back to his brothers on their Wyoming ranch. A great loss. He was good at his job, and he had contacts that we now lack."

"I can get you all the contacts you need,"

Machado promised. He glanced toward the distant hill where the sniper had been emplaced. "First I must deal with Fuentes."

"I didn't hear you say that," Gwen said firmly.

"Nor I," Ramirez echoed.

"Well, I did," Rick replied coldly. "And you're still wanted on kidnapping charges in my country, even though Mrs. Pendleton refuses to press them."

Machado's large eyes widened. "You would turn your own father in to the authorities?"

Rick's eyes narrowed. "The law is the law."

"You keep a book of statutes on your person?" the general asked.

Rick glared at him. "I've been a cop for a long time."

"Amazing. I have spent my life breaking most of the laws that exist, and here I find a son, a stranger, who goes by the book." His eyes narrowed. "I think perhaps they rigged the DNA evidence." He gave the detective a disparaging look. "I would never wear a suit like that, or grow my hair long. You look like a—what is the expression?—a hippie!"

Rick glared at him.

The general glared back.

"Uh, the sniper?" Ramirez reminded them. "He may have gone for reinforcements."

"True." Machado turned to Grange. "Perhaps you should order a sweep on the surrounding hills."

Grange smiled. "I already have."

"Good man. We will soon have a proper government in my country and you will be the commander of the forces in my country."

Ramirez choked. Gwen colored. Rick looked at them, trying to figure out why the hell they were so disturbed.

"We should go," Ramirez said, indicating the car. "I promised her husband that I would have her home very quickly. He might send a search party for us. Not a man to make an enemy of."

"Absolutely," Grange agreed.

"Thank you for making this meeting possible," Machado said, extending his hand to Ramirez.

Ramirez shook it, and then grinned. "It wasn't my idea. I'm related to the president of Mexico. He thought it would be a good idea."

Machado was impressed. "When I retake my country, perhaps you can speak to him for me about a trade agreement."

Ramirez admired the confidence in the other man's voice. "Yes, perhaps I can. Keep well."

"And you."

Gwen and Marquez waved them off before turning back to Machado.

"We should be going, too," Marquez said stiffly. "I have to get back to work."

Machado nodded. He studied his son with curious, strange eyes. "Perhaps, later, we can meet again."

"Perhaps," Rick replied.

"In a place where we do not have to fear an attack from my enemies," Machado said, shaking his head.

"I don't think we can get to Mars yet," Rick quipped.

Machado laughed. "Grange, we should go."

"Yes, sir."

Machado took Gwen's hand and kissed the back of it tenderly. "It has been a pleasure to meet you, *señorita*," he said with pure velvet in his deep voice.

Rick stepped in, took Gwen's hand and pulled her back. He glared at Machado, which made Gwen almost giddy with delight.

Machado's dark eyes twinkled. "So it is like that, huh?"

"Like what?" Rick asked innocently. He dropped Gwen's hand and looked uncomfortable.

"Never mind. I will be in touch."

"Thank you for coming," Gwen told the general.

"It was truly a pleasure." He winked at her, gave Rick a droll look and climbed back into the truck with Grange. They disappeared over the border. Rick stood staring after the truck with mixed feel-ings. Then he turned, said goodbye to the border agent and walked back to his truck with Gwen.

Rick kept to himself for the next couple of days. Gwen didn't intrude. She knew that he was dealing with some emotional issues that he had to resolve in his own mind.

Meanwhile, she went on interviews with neighbors of the murdered college freshman, the case she'd been assigned to as lead detective.

"Did she have any close friends that you know of?" she asked the third neighbor, an elderly woman who seemed to have a whole roomful of cats. They were clean, brushed, well fed and there was no odor, so she must be taking excellent care of them.

"Oh, you've noticed the cats?" the woman asked her with a grin that made her seem years younger. "I'm babysitting."

Gwen blinked. "Excuse me?"

"Babysitting. I have four neighbors with cats, and we've had a problem with animals disappearing around here. So they leave their cats with me while they're at work, and I feed them. It's a nice little windfall for me, since I'm disabled, and the owners have emotional security since they don't have to worry about their furry 'families' going missing."

Gwen laughed. "Impressive."

"Thanks. I love animals. I wish I could afford to keep a cat, but I can't. This is the next best thing."

Gwen noted several pill bottles on the end table by the elderly lady's recliner.

"By the time I pay for all those out of my social

security check," she told Gwen, "there's not much left over for bills and food."

Gwen winced. "That's not right."

The woman sighed. "The economy is terrible. I expect something awful will have to happen to finally set things right." She looked at Gwen over her glasses. "I don't expect to still be around then. But if aliens exist, and they want somebody to experiment on . . ." She raised her hand. "I'm ready to go. To some nice, green planet with lots of meadows and trees and no greedy humans destroying it all for a quick profit."

"You and I would get along," Gwen said with a smile.

The woman nodded. "Now, back to my neighbor. I do keep a watch on the apartment complex, mostly to try to protect myself. I can't fight off an intruder and I don't own a gun. So I make sure I know who belongs here and who doesn't." Her eyes narrowed. "There was a grimy young man with greasy hair who kept coming to see the college girl. She was trying to be nice, you could tell from her expression, but she never let him inside. Once, the last time he came, the police went to her apartment and stayed for several minutes."

Gwen's heart jumped. If there had been police presence, there would be a report, with details of the conversation. She jotted that down on her phone app, making virtual notes.

"That thing is neat," the elderly lady said. "One of my cat-owning friends has one. He can surf the net on it, buy groceries, books, all sorts of things. I never realized we had such things in the modern world. I suppose I live in the past."

Gwen made a mental note to make sure this nice lady got a phone and several phone cards for Christmas, from an anonymous source. It would revolutionize her life.

"Yes, they are quite nice," Gwen said. She smiled. "Thanks for talking to me. You've been a very big help."

"It was my pleasure. I know you young folks don't have much free time, but if you're ever at a loose end, you can come and see me and I'll tell you about the FBI in the seventies."

Gwen stared at her.

"I was a federal agent," the woman told her. "One of the first women in the bureau."

"I would love to hear some stories about those days," Gwen told her. "And I'll make time."

The wrinkled face lit up. "Thank you!"

"No, thank you. I'm fond of pioneers," she replied.

She told Rick about the elderly woman.

"Yes, Evelyn Dorsey." He nodded, smiling. "She's something of a legend over at the FBI field office. Garon Grier goes to see her from time to time." He was the SAC, the special agent in charge, at the San Antonio Field Office now.

"She shot it out with a gang of would-be kidnappers right over on the 410 Loop. Hit two of them before they shot her, almost fatally, and escaped. But she had a description of the car, right down to the license plate number, and she managed to get it out on the radio before she passed out. They nabbed the perps ten miles away. Back in those days, the radio was in the car, not on a belt. It was harder to be in law enforcement."

"I expect so. Ms. Dorsey was very helpful on our college freshman case, by the way. We did have a patrol unit respond to the freshman's call. I'm tracking down the officer who filed the report now."

"I hope we can catch the guy," he replied.

"The cold case unit wants him very badly. They think he's connected to the old case they're working on," she said. "One of those detectives was related to the victim in it."

"Sad."

"Yes." She moved closer to the desk. "You doing okay?"

He grimaced. "No," he said, with a faint smile.

"Why don't you come over and watch the *Twilight* movies with me tonight? We can order a pizza."

He cocked his head and the smile grew. "You know, that sounds like a very good idea."

She grinned. "Glad you think so. I like mushrooms and cheese and pepperoni."

His eyebrows lifted. "Have you been checking out my profile?"

"No. Why?"

"That's my favorite."

She beamed. "Another thing in common."

"We'll find more, I think."

"Yes."

Rick wasn't comfortable with so-called chick
flicks, but he was drawn into the movie almost at
once. He barely noticed when the pizza delivery
girl showed up, and only lifted his hand for the
plate and coffee cup without taking his eyes off
the screen.

Gwen was delighted. It was her favorite film.
She kicked off her shoes and curled up beside him
on the sofa to watch it again, sipping coffee and
munching pizza in a contented silence. It was
amazing, she thought, how comfortable they
were with each other, even at this early stage of
their relationship.

He glanced at her while the vampire was
showing off his skills to the heroine on the screen.
"You're right. This is very good."

"So are the books. I love all of them."

"I guess I'll have to buy them. It isn't often you
find so many likable people in a story chain."

She sipped coffee. "You know, I hadn't
thought of it that way, but you're right. Even the
vampires are likable."

"Odd, isn't it? Likable monsters."

"But they aren't really monsters. They're just misunderstood living-challenged people."

He burst out laughing.

"More pizza?" she asked.

"I think I could hold one more slice."

"Me, too." She jumped up and went to get it.

After they finished eating, she curled up against him through the heroine's introduction to her boyfriend's family, the baseball game in the rain, the arrival of the more dangerous vampires, the heroine's brush with death and, finally, her appearance at the prom in a cast with her boyfriend.

"That was a roller coaster ride," he remarked. "Are there more?"

"Two more. Want to watch the next one?"

He turned toward her, his dark eyes on her radiant face. He pursed his lips. "Yes, I would. But not right now." He pulled her across his lap. "I'm suffering from affection deprivation. Do you think you could assist me?"

"Could I!" she whispered as his mouth came down on hers.

Each kiss became harder, more urgent. As they grew accustomed to the feel and taste of each other, the pleasure grew and it became more difficult to pull back.

He actually groaned when he found himself

lying over her with half their clothes out of the way, just like before. He buried his face in her warm, frantically pulsing throat.

"I'm dying," he ground out.

"Me, too," she whispered back, shivering.

He lifted his head. His eyes were tormented. "How do you feel about marriage?"

She blinked.

He realized that he, the most non-impulsive man on earth, was doing something totally out of character. But he was already crazy about Gwen and the lieutenant was lurking. Even Machado had been giving her long looks. He didn't want her to end up with some other man while he was waiting for the right moment to do something. And besides, he was traditional, so was she, and there was this incredible, almost unbelievable physical compatibility.

He sighed. "Look, we get along very well. We're incredibly suited physically. We have similar jobs, outlooks on life, philosophies, and we're on the same social level. Why don't we drive over the border and get married? Right now. Afterward," he added with a speaking glance, "we can do what we're both dying to do without lingering feelings of guilt."

Her lips parted. She should have challenged that social level comparison immediately, but her body was on fire and all she could think of was relief. She loved him. He was at least fond of her. They both wanted kids. It would work. She would make it work.

"Yes," she blurted out.

He forced himself to get up and he pulled out his cell phone, scrolled down a list of names and punched in a button. "Yes. Ramirez? Sorry to call so late. Can you get me a direct line to the general? I need his help on a—" he glanced at Gwen "—personal matter."

Ramirez sighed. "All right. But you owe me one."

"Yes, I do."

There was a pause, another pause. Rick motioned Gwen for a pencil and paper. He wrote down a number. "Thanks!" he told Ramirez, and hung up. He dialed the number.

"Yes, it's your—" he hesitated "—your son. How do you feel about giving away the bride at a Mexican wedding? Oh, in about thirty minutes."

There was a burst of Spanish from the other end of the line. Rick replied in the same language, protesting that he wasn't up to anything immoral, he was trying to make sure everything was done properly and that meant a proper wedding. The general seemed to calm down. Another hesitation. Rick grinned.

"Thanks," he said, and hung up. He turned to Gwen and pursed his lips. "Do you have a white dress?"

"Do I have a white dress!" she exclaimed, and ran into the next room to put it on.

She left her hair long. The dress was close-fitting, with puffy sleeves and a draped beaded shawl. She looked young and very innocent. And most incredibly sexy.

Rick's body reacted to her visibly. He cleared his throat. "Don't notice that," he said curtly.

"Oh. Okay." She giggled as she joined him and looked up into his dark eyes. "Are you sure?" she asked hesitantly.

He framed her face in his hands and kissed her with breathless tenderness. "I don't know why, but I've never been so sure of anything. No cold feet?"

She shook her head. Her eyes were full of dreams. "Oh, no. Not at all."

He smiled. "Same here. We can share ammunition, too, so it will be cost effective to get married."

She burst out laughing. "I'll be sure to tell my father that when I explain why I didn't invite him to the ceremony."

He grimaced. "I'll have to do the same for my mother. But we don't have time to get them all together. We're eloping."

"Your father will have to be the audience," she said.

"My father." He smiled. "Let's go."

The general was waiting for them at the border. They followed him down a long dusty road to a small village and stopped in front of a mission church with a shiny new bell.

"I donated the bell," the general informed them proudly. "They are good people here, and the priest is a nice young man, from the United States." He hesitated, glancing from one to the other. "I did not think to ask which religious denomination . . . ?"

"Catholic." They both spoke at once, stared at each other, and then burst out laughing.

"We hadn't discussed it before," Rick said.

"Well, it will be good," the general said with a big smile. "Come, the priest is waiting. You two, you're sure about this?"

Gwen looked at Rick with her heart in her eyes. "Very."

"Very, very," Rick added, his dark eyes shining.

"Then we shall proceed."

The general took Gwen down the aisle of the church on his arm. The whole village came to watch, including a number of small children who seemed to find the blonde lady's hair fascinating.

The priest smiled benevolently, read the marriage service. Then they came to the part about a ring.

Rick turned white. "Oh, no."

The general punched him. "Here. I remember everything." He handed him a small circle of gold that looked just right for Gwen's hand.

"Something old. It belonged to my *abuela*," he added, "my grandmother." He smiled. "She would want it to stay in the family."

"It's beautiful," Gwen whispered. "Thank you."

The general nodded. Rick took the small circle of gold and slid it gently onto Gwen's finger, where it was a perfect fit. The priest pronounced them man and wife, and Rick bent to kiss her. And they were married.

Neither of them remembered much about the rest of the evening. Back at Gwen's apartment, there was a feverish removal of cotton and lace, followed by an incredibly long session in bed that left them both covered in sweat, boneless with pleasure and totally exhausted.

Not that exhaustion stopped them. As soon as they were breathing normally again, they reached for each other, and started all over.

"You know, it never occurred to me that marriage would be so much fun," Rick commented when they were finally sleepy.

Gwen, curled up against him, warm and satisfied, laughed softly. "Me, either. I always thought of it as something a little more dignified. You know, for children and . . ." She stopped.

He turned and looked down at her guilty face. "Hey. You want kids. I want kids. What's the problem?"

She relaxed. "You make it seem so simple."

"It is simple. Two people fall in love, get married and have a family." His eyes were on fire with his feelings. "We'll grow old together. But not right away. Maybe not at all," he added worriedly, "when my mother realizes that I got married without even telling her."

"My dad is going to go ballistic, too," she replied. "But he couldn't have come even if I'd had time to ask him. He's tied up with military stuff right now."

"Is he on active duty?"

"Oh, yes," she said, and there was another worry. She still had to tell Rick who her dad was, and all about the family he'd married into. That might be a source of discord. So she wasn't about to face it tonight.

She curled up close and wound her arms around him. "For a guy who never indulged, you're very good."

He laughed. "Compliment returned." He hugged her close. "They said it comes naturally. I guess it does. Of course, there were all these books I read. For educational purposes only."

She grinned. "I read a few of those, too."

He bent and brushed his mouth gently over hers. "I'm glad we waited," he said seriously, searching her eyes. "I know we're out of step with the world. But I don't care. This was right for us."

"Yes, it was. Thank you for having enough

restraint," she added. "We couldn't have counted on me for it. I was on fire!"

"So was I. But I was thinking about later, generations later, when we tell our grandchildren and great-grandchildren about how it was when we fell in love and got married." He closed his eyes. "It's a golden memory. Not a legalization of something that had gone on before."

She pressed her mouth into his warm, muscular shoulder with a smile. "And the nicest thing is that you're already my best friend."

"You're mine, too." He kissed her hair. "Go to sleep. We'll get up tomorrow and face the music."

"What?"

"I was just thinking," he mused, "that the lieutenant is going to foam at the mouth when we tell him."

"What?" she exclaimed.

"Just a hunch." He thought the lieutenant had a case on Gwen. Maybe, maybe not. But he was expecting fireworks the next day.

CHAPTER 9

>————<

"Fireworks" was, if anything, an understatement.

"You're married?" Lieutenant Hollister exclaimed.

Gwen moved a little closer to Rick. "Yes. Sorry, we would have invited you, but we didn't want the expense of a big wedding, so we eloped," she told him, stretching the truth.

"Eloped." Hollister leaned back in his chair with a grumpy sigh. He glared at Marquez. "Well, it was certainly quick."

"We knew how we felt at once," Rick replied with a smile at his wife. "No sense having a long engagement."

She smiled back. "Absolutely."

"Well, congratulations," Hollister said after a minute. He got up, smiled and shook hands with both of them. "How did your mother take it?" he asked Rick.

Rick grimaced. "Haven't told her."

"Why don't you two take the day off and call it a honeymoon," Hollister suggested. "Gail Rogers can sub for you," he told Rick. "I don't want

Barbara coming after me with a bazooka because she heard the news from somebody else."

"Good idea," Rick said. "Thanks!"

"My pleasure. A wedding present. A short one," he added. "You have to be back on the job tomorrow. And when are we losing you?" he asked Gwen.

She wasn't sure what he meant, and then she realized that she belonged to a federal agency. "I'm not sure. I'll have to talk to my boss and he'll have to discuss it with the captain here."

Hollister nodded. "You've done very well. I'll be sorry to lose you."

She smiled. "I'll be sorry to go. I may have to make some minor adjustments in my career path, as well," she added with a worried glance at Rick. "I don't really want to keep a job that sends me around the world every other week. Not now."

Hollister pursed his lips. "We can always use another detective," he pointed out. "You'd pick it back up in no time, and we have all sorts of workshops and training courses."

She beamed. "You mean it?"

"Of course," he assured her.

"Wait a minute, you'd give up working for the feds, for me?" Rick asked, as if he couldn't quite believe it.

"I would," she said solemnly. "I'm tired of living out of a suitcase. And I really like San Antonio." She didn't add that she was also very

180

tired of the D.C. social scene and being required to hostess parties for her dad. It was never enjoyable. She didn't like crowds or parties. To give him his due, neither did her father. But he was certainly going to be in the center of the Washington social whirl very soon. She dreaded having to tell Rick about it.

"Well," Rick said, and couldn't resist a charming smile.

She laughed. "And now for the really hard part. We have to break the news to your mother."

"She'll kill me," he groaned.

"No. We'll take her a pot of flowers," Gwen said firmly. "She's a gardener. I know she wouldn't mind a bribe that she could plant."

They all laughed.

And actually, Barbara wasn't mad. She burst into tears, hugged them both and rambled on for several minutes about how depressed she'd been that women never seemed to see Rick as a potential mate as much as a shoulder to cry on.

"I'm just so happy!"

"I'm so glad," Gwen enthused. "But we still brought you a bribe."

"A bribe?" Barbara asked, wiping away tears.

Gwen went onto the porch and came back inside carrying a huge potted plant.

"It's an umbrella plant!" Barbara exclaimed. "I've wanted one for years, but I could never find one the right size. It's perfect!"

"I thought you could plant it," Gwen said.

"Oh, no, I'll let it live inside. I'll put grow lights around it and fertilize it and . . ." She hesitated. "You two didn't have to get married?"

They howled.

"She's as Victorian as we are," Rick told his mother with a warm smile.

"That's wonderful! Welcome to the stone age, my dear!" she told Gwen and hugged her, hard.

"Where are you going to live? In San Antonio?" Barbara asked, resigned.

Gwen and Rick had discussed this. "The old Andrews place is up for sale, right in downtown Jacobsville," Rick said, "next door to the Griers. In fact, I put in an offer for it this morning."

"Oh!" Barbara started crying again. "I thought you'd want to live where your jobs are."

Explanation about Gwen's job could come later, Rick decided. "We want to live near you," Rick replied.

"Because when the kids come along," Gwen added with a grin, "you'll want to be able to see them."

Barbara felt her forehead. "Maybe I'm feverish. You want to have kids?"

"Oh, yes," Gwen replied, smiling.

"Lots of kids," Rick added.

"I can buy a toy store," Barbara murmured to herself. "But first I need to stock up on organic seeds, so that I can make healthy stuff for the baby."

"We just got married yesterday," Rick pointed out.

"That's right, and this is November." She went looking for a calendar. "And nine months from now is harvest season!" she called back.

Rick and Gwen shook their heads.

They stayed for supper, a delicious affair, and then settled down to watch the news. Gwen, sitting contentedly beside her husband, had no warning of what was about to happen.

A newscaster smiled as a picture of a four-star general, very well-known to the public, was splashed across the screen. "And this just in. Amid rumors that he was retiring or resigning from the service, we have just learned that General David Cassaway, former U.S. Commander in Iraq, has been named director of the Central Intelligence Agency. General Cassaway, a former covert ops commander, has commanded American troops in Iraq for the past two years. He was rumored to be retiring from the military, but it seems that he was only considering a new job."

Barbara glanced at Gwen. "Why, what a coincidence. That's your last name."

The newscaster was adding, "General Cassaway's only son, Larry, died in a classified operation in the Middle East just a few months ago. We wish General Cassaway the best of luck in his new position. Now for other news . . ."

Rick was staring at Gwen as if she'd grown horns. "Your brother's name was Larry, wasn't it?" he asked. "The one who was killed in action?"

Barbara was staring. So was Rick.

Gwen took a deep breath. "He's my father," she confessed.

Rick wasn't handling this well. "Your father is the new head of the CIA?"

"Well, sort of," she said, nodding worriedly.

Rick knew about Washington society from people in his department who had to deal with the socialites in D.C. He was certain that there were no poor generals in the military, and the head of the CIA would certainly not be in line for food stamps.

"What sort of place do you live in, when you go home?" Rick asked very quietly.

Gwen sighed. "We have a big house in Maryland, on several acres of land. My dad likes horses. He raises, well, thoroughbreds." She was almost cringing by now.

"And drives a . . . ?"

She swallowed. "Jaguar."

Rick got up and turned away with an exasperated sigh. "Why didn't you tell me?"

"Because I was afraid you'd do just what you're doing now," Gwen moaned. "Judging me by the company I keep. I hate parties. I hate receptions. I hate hostessing! I'm perfectly happy working a federal job, or a police job, any sort of job that doesn't require me to put on an evening gown and look rich!"

"Rich." Rick ran his fingers through his hair.

"I'm not rich," she pointed out.

"But your father is."

She grimaced. "He was born into one of the founding families. He went to Harvard, and then to West Point," she said. "But he's just a regular person. He doesn't put on airs."

"Sure."

"Rick—" she got up and went to him "—I'm not my family. I don't have money. I work for my living. For heaven's sake, this suit is a year old!"

He turned around. His face was hard. "My suit is three years old," he said stiffly. "I drive a pickup truck. I can barely afford tickets to the theater."

She gave him a strained look. "You'll get used to this," she promised him. "It will just take a little time. You've had one too many upsets in the past few weeks."

He sighed heavily. "We should have waited to get married," he ground out.

"No," she returned. "If we'd waited and you'd found out, you'd never have married me at all."

Before Rick could open his mouth and destroy his future, Barbara got up and stood between them. "She's right," she told her son. "You need to stop before you say something you'll regret. Let Gwen go home for tonight, and you sleep on it. Things will look better in the morning." She went to get her cell phone and dialed a number. She waited until the call was answered. "Cash? Gwen Cassaway's going back to San Antonio for the night and I don't want her driving up there alone, do you have someone who can take her?"

"No . . . !" Gwen protested.

Barbara held up a hand. She grinned. "I thought you might. Thanks! I owe you a nice apple pie." She hung up. "One of Cash's men lives in San Antonio and he's on his way home. He'll swing by and give you a lift. He won't mind, and he's very nice. His name is Carlton Ames. He'll take good care of you."

Rick was cursing himself for not letting Gwen drive her car down instead of insisting that she come with him. He didn't like the idea of her riding with another man. They were married. At least, temporarily.

"Go home and don't worry," Barbara said, hugging her. "It will be all right."

Gwen managed a smile. She looked at Rick, but he wouldn't meet her eyes. She drew in a long breath and put on her coat and picked up her purse. She walked out to the front porch with Barbara, who closed the door behind them.

"He's still upset about meeting his father,"

Barbara said gently. "He'll get over this. You just get a good night's sleep and don't worry. It will work out. I'm so happy he married you!" She hugged the younger woman again. "You're going to be very happy together once he gets over the shock."

"I hope you're right. I should have told him. I was afraid to."

"Have you talked to your father?"

She shook her head. "I have to do that tonight." She grimaced. "He's not going to be happy, either."

"Does he have prejudices . . . ?" Barbara worried at once.

Gwen laughed. "Heavens, no! Dad docsn't see color or race or religion. He's very liberal. No, he'll be hurt that I didn't tcll him first."

"That's all right then. You'll make it up with him. And with Rick. Oh, there's Carlton!"

She waved as an off-duty police car pulled up at the porch. A nice young man got out and smiled. "I'm going to have company for the ride, I hear?" he asked.

"Yes, this is my new daughter-in-law, Gwen." Barbara introduced them. "That's Carlton," she added with a grin. "She didn't drive her own car and she has to get back to San Antonio to pick it up. Thanks for giving her a ride."

"Should I follow you back down here, then?" he offered.

Gwen shook her head. "I have things to get together in my apartment. But thanks."

"No problem. Shall we go?"

Gwen looked toward the porch, but the door was still closed. She saw Barbara wince. She managed a smile. "I'll see you later, then," she said. "Have a good night."

"You, too, dear," Barbara said. She forced a smile. "Good night."

She watched them leave. Then she went back in the house and closed the door. "Rick?"

He was on the phone. She wondered who he could be calling at this hour of the night. Perhaps it was work.

He hung up and came into the living room, looking more unapproachable than she'd ever seen him. "I'm going for a drive. I won't be long."

"She was very upset," she said gently. "She can't help who her father is, any more than you can."

He looked torn. "I know that. But she should have told me."

"I think she was afraid to. She's very much in love, you know."

He flushed and looked away. "I won't be long."

She watched him go, feeling a new and bitter distance between them, something she'd never felt before. She hoped they could work things out. She liked Gwen a lot.

• • •

Rick pulled up to the country bar, locked the truck and walked inside. It was late and there were only a couple of cowboys sitting in booths. A man in the back motioned to Rick, who walked down the aisle to sit across from him.

The older man gave him an amused smile. "Should I be flattered that you called me when you needed sympathy? Why not talk to your mother?"

Rick sighed. "It's not really something a woman would understand," he muttered.

General Machado pursed his lips. "No? Perhaps not." He motioned to the waiter, who came over at once, grinning. "Coffee for my young friend, please."

"At once!"

Rick's eyebrows arched at the man's quick manner.

"He wants to go and help liberate my country," Machado told Rick with a grin. "I have the ability to inspire revolutions."

"I noticed," Rick said dryly.

General Emilio Machado leaned back against the booth, studying the young man who looked so much like himself. "You know, we do favor each other."

"A bit."

The waiter came back with the coffee, placing a mug in front of Rick, along with small

189

containers of cream and sugar, and a spoon. "Anything else for you, sir?" he asked the general with respect.

"No, that will do for now, thank you."

"A pleasure! If you need anything, just call."

"I will."

The waiter scampered away. Machado watched Rick sip hot coffee. "Just married, and already you quarrel?"

"She lied to me. Well, she lied by omission," he corrected coolly.

"About what?"

"It turns out that her father is the new head of the CIA."

"Ah, yes, General Cassaway. He and Grange are friends."

Rick recalled an odd conversation that Gwen and Grange had shared at the first meeting with Machado at the border. It had puzzled him at the time. Now he knew that she had been cautioning Grange not to give away her identity. It made him even sadder.

"He's rich," Rick said curtly.

"And you are not." Machado understood the problem. "Does it matter so much, if you care for the woman? What if it was your mother who was wealthy, and her father who was poor?"

He shifted restlessly. "I don't know."

"But of course you do. You would not care."

Rick sipped more coffee. He was losing the argument.

Machado toyed with his own cup. "I was a millionaire, in my country," he confided. "I had everything a man could possibly want, right down to a Rolls-Royce and a private helicopter. Perhaps I had too much, and God resented the fact that I spent more money on me than I did on the poor villagers who were being displaced and murdered by my underling's minions as he worked to bring in foreign oil corporations. The oil and natural gas are quite valuable, and the villagers considered them a nuisance that interfered with the fishing." He smiled. "They have no interest in great wealth. They live from day to day, quietly, with no clocks, no super-markets, no strip malls. Perhaps they have the right idea, and the rest of the world has gone insane from this disease called civilization."

Rick smiled back. "It would be a less hectic life."

"Yes, indeed." His dark eyes were thoughtful. "I was careless. I will never be careless again. And the man who usurped my place and made my people suffer will pay a very high price for his arrogance and greed, I promise you." The look on his face gave Rick cold chills.

"We've heard what he did to private citizens," Rick agreed.

"That is my fault. I should have listened. A . . .

friend of mine, an archaeologist, tried to warn me about what his people were doing to the native tribes. I thought she was overstating, trying to get me to clamp down on foreign interests in the name of preserving archaeological treasures."

"A female archaeologist?"

He chuckled. "There are many these days. Yes, she taught at a small college in the United States. She was visiting my country when she stumbled onto a find so amazing that she hesitated to even announce it before she had time to substantiate her claim with evidence." His face hardened. "There was gossip that they put her in prison. I shudder to think what might have been done to her. That will be on my soul forever, if she was harmed."

"Maybe she escaped," Rick said, trying to find something comforting to say. "Rumors and gossip are usually pretty far off the mark."

"You think so?" Machado's dark eyes were sad but hopeful.

"Anything is possible."

Machado sighed. "I suppose."

The waiter came scurrying up looking worried. "El General, there is a police car coming this way," he said excitedly.

Machado looked at Rick.

"I'm not involved in any attempts to kidnap or arrest you," he said dryly.

"Is the car local?" Machado asked.

"Yes. It is a Jacobsville police car."

Machado weighed his options. While he was trying to decide whether to make a break out the back door, a tall, imposing man in a police uniform with large dark eyes and his long hair in a ponytail came in the door, looked around and spotted Rick with the general.

Rick relaxed. "It's all right," he said. "That's Cash Grier."

"You know him?"

"Yes. He's our police chief. He's a good man. Used to be a government assassin, or that's the rumor," Rick mused.

Machado laughed under his breath.

Cash walked over to their table. He wasn't smiling. "I'm afraid I have some bad news."

"You're here to arrest me?" Machado asked dryly.

Cash glanced at him. "Have you broken the law?" he asked curiously. It was obvious that he didn't recognize the bar's famous patron.

"Not lately," Machado lied.

Cash looked back at Rick, who was going tense.

"Gwen," he burst out.

Cash grimaced. "I'm afraid so. There's been a wreck . . ."

Rick was out of the booth in a flash. "How badly is she hurt?" he asked at once, white-faced. "Is she all right?"

"They've transported her and Ames to

Jacobsville General," he said quietly. "Ames is pretty bad. Ms. Cassaway has at the very least a broken rib . . . !" Rick was already out of the bar, running for his truck.

"Wait! I'm coming with you!" Machado called after him, and stopped just long enough to pay the waiter, who bowed respectfully.

Cash, confused by the two men, got back in his patrol car and followed the pickup truck down the long road to the hospital. To his credit, he didn't pull out his ticket book when he pulled in behind Rick at the emergency entrance.

"My wife, Gwen Cassaway," Rick told the clerk at the desk. "They just brought her in."

The clerk studied him. "Oh, that's you, Detective Marquez," she said, smiling. "Yes, and she's your wife? Congratulations! Yes, she's in X-ray right now. Dr. Coltrain is treating her . . ."

"Copper or Lou?" Rick asked, because the married Coltrains were both doctors.

"Lou," came the reply.

"Thanks."

"You can have a seat right over there," the clerk said gently, "and I'll have someone ask Dr. Coltrain to come see you, okay?"

Rick wanted to rush behind the counter, but he knew better. He ground his teeth together. "Okay."

"Be just a sec." The clerk picked up the phone.

"She will be all right," Machado told his son

with a warm smile. "She has great courage for one so young."

Rick felt rocked to the soles of his feet. He never should have reacted as he had. He'd upset her. But . . . she hadn't been driving, and Ames was one of Cash's better drivers . . .

He turned to the police chief. "Ames wrecked the car? How?"

"That's what I'd like to know," Cash said curtly. "There was another set of tracks in the dirt nearby, as if a car had sideswiped them. I've got men tracking right now."

"If you need help, I can provide a tracker who might even excel your own," Machado offered quietly.

Cash had been sizing the other man up. He pursed his lips. "You look familiar."

"There are very few photographs of me," Machado replied.

"Yes, but we've met. I can't remember where. Maybe it will come back to me."

Machado raised an eyebrow. "It would be just as well if your memory lapses for the next few hours. My son can use the company."

"Your son?" Cash's dark eyes narrowed on the older man. "Machado."

The older man nodded and smiled.

"Gwen had a photo of you. I had to break the news to Rick's mother, about your connection to him."

"Ah, yes, that was how he was told. Ingenious." The general's expression sombered. "I hope she and the officer will be all right."

"So do I," Cash said. "I can't help being concerned about that other car."

Machado came a step closer. "The Fuentes bunch have much reason to interfere with my plans. They are being paid by my successor to spy on me. There is also a very high level mole in the DEA. I do not know who it is," he added. "But even I am aware of him."

"Damn," Cash muttered.

"Yes, things are quite complicated. I did not mean to involve the children in my war," he added, with a rueful glance at Rick, who was pacing the floor.

"No parent would. Sometimes fate intervenes. Her father should be told."

"Yes," Machado replied. "He should." He excused himself and spoke to Rick.

"Her father." Rick groaned. "How am I going to find him?"

Machado grinned. "I think I can solve that problem." He pulled out his disposable cell phone, one of many, and dialed a number. "Grange? Yes. Gwen has been injured in an automobile accident. I need you to call her father and tell him. We don't know details yet. She has at least a broken rib. The rest we don't know . . . but he should come."

There was a pause. "Yes. Thank you. She is at the Jacobsville hospital. Yes. All right." He hung up. "Grange and her father are friends. He will make the call."

Rick averted his eyes. "Hell of a way to meet in-laws," he muttered.

"I do agree," Machado said. He put an affectionate arm around his son's neck. "But you will get through it. Come. Sit down and stop pacing, before you wear a hole in the floor."

Rick allowed himself to be led to a chair. It was kind of nice, having a father.

Dr. Louise Coltrain came into the room in her white lab coat, smiling. She was introduced to Gwen's husband and father-in-law with some surprise, because no one locally knew about the wedding.

"Congratulations," she told Rick. "She'll be all right," she added quickly. "She does have a broken rib, but the other injuries are mostly bruises. Patrolman Ames has a head injury," she told Cash. "His prognosis is going to be trickier. I'm having him airlifted to San Antonio, to the Marshall Center. He's holding his own so far, though. Do you have a way to notify his family?"

Cash shook his head. "He doesn't have any family that I'm aware of. Just me," he added with a grim smile. "So I'm the one to notify."

She nodded. "I'll keep you in the loop. Detective

Marquez, you can see your wife now. I'll take you back . . ."

"Where the hell is my daughter?"

Rick felt a shiver go down his spine. That voice, deep and cold with authority, froze everyone in the waiting room. Rick turned to find the face that went with it, and understood at once how this man had risen to become a four-star general. He was in full uniform, every button polished, his hat at the perfect angle, his hard face almost bristling with antagonism, his black eyes glittering with it.

"And who's responsible for putting her in the hospital?" he added in a tone that was only a little less intimidating.

While Rick was working on an answer, Barbara came in the door, worried and unsettled by his call. She paused beside the military man who was raising Cain in the waiting room.

"My goodness, someone had his razor blade soup this morning, I see!" she exclaimed with pure hostility. "Now you calm down and stop shouting at people. This is a hospital, not a military installation!"

CHAPTER 10

General Cassaway turned and looked down at the willowy blonde woman who was glaring up at him.

"Who the hell are you?" he demanded.

"The woman who's going to have you arrested if you don't calm down," she replied. "Rick, how is she?" she asked, holding out her arms.

Rick came and held her close. "Broken rib," he said. "And some bruising. She'll be all right."

"Who are you?" General Cassaway demanded.

Rick turned. "I'm Gwen's husband. Detective Sergeant Rick Marquez," he said coldly, not backing down an inch.

"Her husband?"

"Yes. And he's my son," Barbara added.

"And also my son," General Machado said, joining them. He smiled at Barbara, who smiled back.

"You two are married?" Cassaway asked.

Barbara laughed. "No. He's much too young for me," she said.

Machado gave her an amused look. "I do like older women," he admitted.

She just shook her head.

"I want to see my daughter," Cassaway told Lou Coltrain.

"Of course. Come this way. You, too, Rick."

Cassaway was surprised at the first name basis.

"We all know each other here," Lou told him. "I'm a newcomer, so to speak, but my husband is from here. He's known Rick since Barbara adopted him."

"I see."

Gwen was heavily sedated, but her eyes opened and she brightened when she saw her husband and her father walk into the recovery room.

"Dad! Rick!"

Rick went on one side to take a hand, her father on the other.

"I'm so sorry," she began.

"Don't be absurd." Rick kissed her forehead. "I was an idiot. I'm sorry! I never should have let you go with Ames."

"Ames! How is he?" she asked. "The other car came out of nowhere! We didn't even see it until it hit us. There were three men in it . . ."

"Did you recognize any of them?"

"No," she replied. "But it could have been Fuentes. The last of the living brothers, the drug lords."

"By God, I'll have them hunted down like rats," Cassaway said icily.

"My father will beat you to it," Rick replied coolly.

"Just who is your father?" Cassaway asked suddenly. "He looks very familiar."

"General Emilio Machado," Rick said, and with a hint of pride that reflected in the tilt of his chin.

Cassaway pursed his lips. "Grange's boss. Yes, we know about that upcoming operation. We can't be involved, of course."

"Of course," Rick replied with twinkling eyes.

"But we are rooting for the good guys," came the amused comment.

Rick chuckled.

"So you're married," Cassaway said. He shook his head. "Your mother would have loved seeing you married." He winced. "I would have, too."

"I'm so sorry," she said. "But I hadn't told Rick who you were." She bit her lip.

"What did that have to do with anything?" the older man asked, puzzled.

"I'm a city detective," Rick said sardonically. "I wear three-year-old suits and I drive a pickup truck."

"Hell, I drive a pickup truck, too," the general said, shrugging. "So what?"

Rick liked the man already. He grinned.

"See?" Gwen asked her husband. "I told you he wasn't what you thought."

"Snob," the general said, glaring at Rick. "I don't pick my friends for their bank accounts."

"Sorry," Rick said. "I didn't know you."

"You'll get there, son."

"Congratulations on the appointment," Rick said.

The general shrugged. "I don't know how long I'll last. I don't kiss butt, if you know what I mean, and I say what I think. Not very popular to speak your mind sometimes."

"I think honesty never goes out of style, and has value," Rick replied.

The general's eyes twinkled. "You did good," he told his daughter.

She just smiled.

Out in the waiting room, Cash Grier was talking on the phone to someone in San Antonio while the general thumbed through a magazine. Barbara paced, worried. Gwen's father was a hard case. She hoped he and Rick would learn to get along.

Cash closed his flip phone grimly. "They found a car, abandoned, a few miles outside of Comanche Wells," he said. "We can't say for sure that it's the one that hit Ames, but it has black paint on the fender, and Ames's car is black. We ran wants and warrants on it—it was stolen."

"Fuentes," Machado said quietly. His dark eyes narrowed. "I have had just about enough of him. I think he will have to meet with a similar accident soon."

"I didn't hear you say that," Cash told him.

"Did I say something?" Machado asked.

"Why, I was simply voicing a prediction."

"Terroristic threats and acts," he said, waving a finger at Machado. "And I'm conveniently forgetting your connection with the Pendleton kidnapping for the next hour or so. After that," he added with pursed lips, "things could get interesting here."

Machado grinned. "I will be long gone by then. My son needed me."

Cash smiled. "I have a daughter," he said. "She's going on three years old. Red hair and green eyes and a temper worse than mine."

"I would like to have known my son when he was small," Machado said sadly. "I did not know about him. Dolores kept her secret all the way to the grave. A pity."

"It was nice for me, that you didn't know," Barbara said gently. "When I adopted him, he gave me a reason to live." She stood up. "Do you think things happen for a reason?" she asked philosophically.

"Yes, I do," Machado replied with a smile. "Perhaps fate had a hand in all this."

"Well, I suppose . . ." she began.

"I have to get back home," General Cassaway was saying as he walked out with Rick. "But it's been a pleasure meeting you, son." He shook hands with Rick.

"Same here," Rick told him. "I'll take better care of your daughter from now on. And I won't be so inflexible next time she springs a surprise on me," he added with a laugh.

"See that you aren't. Remember what I do for a living now," he told the younger man with a grin. "I can find you anywhere, anytime."

"Yes, sir," Rick replied.

The general turned to Machado. "And you'd better hightail it out of Mexico pretty soon," he said in a confidential tone. "Things are going to heat up in Sonora. A storm's coming. You don't want to be in its way."

Machado nodded. "Thank you."

"Oh, I have ulterior motives," Cassaway assured him. "I want that rat out of Barrera before he turns your country into the world's largest cocaine distribution center."

"So do I," Machado replied quietly. "I promise you, his days of power will soon come to an end."

"Wish I could help," Cassaway told him. "But I think you have enough intel and mercs to do the job."

"Including a friend of yours," Machado replied, smiling.

"A very good one. He'll get the job done." He shook hands with Machado. Then he turned to Barbara. "You've got a smart mouth on you."

She glared at him. "And you've got a sharp tongue on you."

He smiled. "I like pepper."

She shifted. "Me, too."

"She's a great cook," Rick said, sliding his arm around her shoulders. "She owns the local café here, and does most of the cooking for it."

"Really! I'm something of a chef myself," Cassaway replied. "I grow my own vegetables and I get a local grandmother to come over and help me can every summer."

Barbara moved closer. "I can, too. I like to dry herbs as well."

"Now I've got a herb garden of my own," the general said. "But it isn't doing as well as I'd like."

"Do you have a composter?" Barbara asked.

His eyebrows lifted. "A what?"

"A composter, for organic waste from the kitchen." She went on to explain to him how it worked and what you did with it.

"A fellow gardener," Cassaway said with a beaming smile. "What a surprise! So few women garden these days."

"Oh, we have plenty around Jacobsville who plant gardens," Barbara said. "You'll have to come and visit us next summer. I can show you how to grow corn ten feet high, even in a drought," she added.

Cassaway moved a step closer. He was huge, Barbara thought, tall and good-looking and built like a tank. He had thick black hair and black eyes and a tan complexion. Nice mouth.

Cassaway was thinking the same thing about

Barbara. She was tall and willowy and very pretty.

"I might visit sooner than that," he said in a low, deep tone. "Is there a hotel?"

"Yes, but I have a big Victorian house. Rick and Gwen can stay there, too. We'll have a family reunion." She flushed a little, and laughed, and then looked at Machado. "That invitation includes you, also," she added. "If you're through with your revolution by then," she said ruefully.

"I think that is a good possibility, and I will accept the invitation," Machado said. He kissed her hand and bowed. "Thank you for taking such good care of my son."

She smiled. "He's been the joy of my life. I had nobody until Rick needed a home."

"I only have a daughter," General Cassaway said sadly. "I lost my son earlier this year to an IED, and my wife died some years ago."

"I'm so sorry," Barbara said with genuine sympathy. "I miscarried the only child I ever had. It must be terrible to lose one who's grown."

"Worse than death," Cassaway agreed. He cleared his throat and looked away. He drew in a long breath. "Well, my adjutant is doing the ants' dance, so I guess we'd better go," he said, nodding toward a young officer standing in the doorway.

"The ants' dance?" Barbara asked.

"He moves around like that when he's in a hurry to do something, like he's got ants climbing his legs. Good man, but a little testy." He shrugged. "Like me. He suits me." He shook hands with Rick. "I've heard good things about you from Grange. Your police chief over there—" he nodded toward Cash, who was talking on the phone again "—speaks highly of you."

Rick smiled. "Nice to know. I love my job. I like to think I'm good at it."

"Take care of my little girl."

"You know I will."

He paused at Barbara and looked down at her with quiet admiration. "And I'll see you later."

She grinned. "Okay!"

He nodded at the others, and walked toward the young man, who was now motioning frantically.

Cash joined them a minute later. "Sorry, I wasn't trying to be rude. I've got a man working on the hit-and-run, and I've been checking in. There was an incident at the border crossing over near Del Rio," he added. "Three men jumped a border agent, knocked him out and took off over the crossing into Mexico. We think it was the same men who ran Ames off the road."

"Great," Rick muttered. "Just great. Now we work on trying to get them extradited back to the States. That will be good for a year, even if we can get a positive identification of who they are."

Machado pursed his lips. "I would not worry about that. Such men are easy to find, for a good tracker, and equally easy to deal with."

"I didn't hear that," Cash said.

Machado chuckled. "Of course not. I was, again, making a prediction."

"Thanks for coming with me," Rick told Machado. "And for the shoulder earlier."

Machado embraced his son in a bear hug. "I will always be around, whenever you need me." He searched the younger man's face. "I am very proud to have such a man for my son."

Rick swallowed hard. "I'm proud to have such a man for my father."

Machado's eyes were suspiciously bright. He laughed suddenly. "We will both be wailing in another minute. I must go. Grange is waiting for me in the parking lot."

"I can't say anything officially," Cash told the general. "But privately, I wish you good luck."

Machado shook his hand. "Thank you, my friend. I hope your patrolman will be all right."

"So do I," Cash said.

Rick walked Machado to the door. Outside, Winslow Grange was sitting behind the wheel of Machado's pickup truck, waiting.

Machado turned to his son. "When the time comes, I will be happy to let you become my liaison with the American authorities. And it will come," he added solemnly. "My country has many resources that will appeal to outside interests. I would prefer to deal with republics or democracies rather than totalitarian states."

"A wise decision," Rick said. "And when the time comes, I'll be here."

Machado smiled. *"Que vayas con Dios, mi hijo,"* he said, using the familiar tense that was only applied to family and close friends.

It made Rick feel warm inside, that his father already felt affection for him. He waved as the two men in the truck departed. He hoped his father wouldn't get killed in the attempt to retake Barrera. But, then, Machado was a general, and he'd won the title fairly, in many battles. He would be all right. Rick was certain of it.

Gwen came home two days later. She wore a rib belt and winced every time she moved. The lieutenant had granted her sick leave, but she was impatient to get back on the job. Rick had to make threats to keep her in bed at all, at Barbara's house.

"And I'm a burden on your poor mother," Gwen protested. "She has a business to run, and here she is bringing me food on trays . . . !"

"She doesn't mind," Rick assured her.

"Of course she doesn't mind," Barbara said as she brought in soup and crackers. "She's working on planning a fantastic Thanksgiving dinner in a couple of weeks. I'm going to invite your father," she told Gwen and then flushed a little. "I guess that would be all right. I don't know," she hesitated, looking around her. "He's head of the CIA and used to crystal and fine china . . ."

"He doesn't use the good place settings at home," Gwen said dryly. "He likes plain white ceramic plates and thick Starbucks coffee mugs and just plain fare to eat. He isn't a fancy mannered person, although he can blend into high society when he has to. He'll think of it as a welcome relief from the D.C. whirl. Which I'm happy to be out of," she added heavily. "I never liked having to hostess parties. I like working in law enforcement."

"Me, too," Rick said, smiling warmly at his wife. "I'm just sorry about what happened to you and Ames."

"Yes. Have we heard anything about Ames?"

"Cash Grier said that he regained consciousness this morning," Barbara said with a smile. "It's all coming back to him. He remembered what the men looked like. He got a better view of them than you did," she told the younger woman. "He recognized Fuentes."

"Fuentes himself?" Gwen was shocked. "Why would he do his own dirty work?"

"Fuentes knows that you're married to me, and that I'm General Machado's son," Rick said somberly. "I think he was trying to get back at the general, in a roundabout way. He may have thought it was me driving. He wouldn't have known that you were with Ames."

"Yes," Barbara said worriedly. "And he may

try again. You can't go anywhere alone from now on, at least until Fuentes is arrested."

"He won't be," Rick said coldly. "Dozens of policemen have tried to pin him down, nobody has succeeded. He has a hideout in the mountains and guards at every checkpoint. An undercover agent died trying to infiltrate his camp a few weeks ago. I'd love to see him behind bars. It's trying to get him there that's the problem."

"Well, your father's not too happy with him right now," Barbara remarked.

"And the general has ways and means that we don't have access to," Gwen agreed.

"True," Rick said.

"I think we may hear some good news soon about Fuentes and his bunch," Barbara said. "But for now, my main focus is getting your wife back on her feet," she told her son. "Good food and a little spoiling always does the trick."

"You're a nice mother," Rick said.

"A very nice mother and I'm so happy that you're going to be mine, too," Gwen told her with a warm smile. She shifted in the bed and groaned.

"Time for meds," Barbara said, and went out to get them.

Rick bent and kissed Gwen gently between her eyes. "You get better," he whispered. "I have erotic plans for you at some future time very soon."

She laughed, wincing, and lifted her mouth to touch his. "You aren't the only one with plans. Darn this rib!"

"Bad timing, and Fuentes's fault," Rick murmured as he brushed her mouth tenderly with his. "But we have forever."

"Yes," she whispered, beaming. "Forever."

Thanksgiving came suddenly and with, of all things, snow! Rick and Gwen walked out into the yard at Barbara's house and laughed as it piled down on the bare limbs of the trees around the fence line.

"Snow!" she exclaimed. "I didn't know it snowed in Texas!"

"Hey, it snowed in South Africa twice in August," he pointed out. "The weather is loopy."

She smiled and hugged him, still wincing a little, because her rib was tender. She was healing quickly, though. Soon, she would be whole again and ready for more amorous adventures with her new husband.

"Is your father coming down?" he asked Gwen.

"Oh, yes. He said he wouldn't miss a home-made Thanksgiving dinner for the world. He can cook, but he hates doing it on holidays, and he mostly eats out. He's very excited. And not only about the meal," she added with an impish grin. "I think he likes your mother."

"Wouldn't that be a match?" he mused.

"Yes, it would. They're both alone and about the same age. Dad's quite a guy."

"But he's head of a federal agency. He lives in D.C. and she owns a restaurant here," Rick pointed out.

"If they really want to, they'll find a way."

"I guess so." He turned to her, in the white flaky curtain, and drew her gently to his chest. "The best thing I ever did in life was marry you," he said somberly. "I may not say it a lot but I love you very much."

She caught her breath at the tenderness in his deep voice. "I love you, too," she whispered back.

He bent and drew her mouth under his, teasing the upper lip with his tongue, parting her lips so that his could cover them hungrily. He forgot everything in the flashpoint heat of desire. His arms closed around her, enveloping her so tightly that she moaned.

He heard that, and drew back at once. "Sorry," he said quickly. "I forgot!"

She laughed breathily. "It's okay. I forgot, too. Just another week or two, and I'll be in fine shape."

He lifted an eyebrow and looked down at her trim, curvy body in jeans and a tight sweater. "I'll say you're in fine shape," he murmured dryly.

"Oh, you!" She punched him lightly in the chest.

"Shapely, sexy and sweet. I'm a lucky man."

She reached up and kissed him back. "We're both lucky."

He sighed. "I suppose we should go back inside and offer to peel potatoes."

"I suppose so."

He kissed her again, smiling. "In a minute."

She sighed. "Yes. In a minute . . . or two . . . or three . . ."

Ten minutes later, they went back inside. Barbara gave them an amused look and handed Rick a huge pan full of potatoes and a paring knife. He sighed and got to work.

The general came with an entourage, but they were housed in the local hotel in Jacobsville. General Cassaway did allow his adjutant and a clerk to move into Barbara's house with him, with her permission of course, and he had a case full of electronic equipment that had to find living space as well.

"I have to keep in touch with everyone in my department, monitor the web, answer queries, inform the proper people at Homeland Security about my activities," the general said, rattling off his duties. "It's a great job, but it takes most of my time. That's why I've been remiss in the email department," he added with a smile at Gwen.

"I think you do very well, considering how little free time you have, Dad," she told him.

"Thanks." He dug into the dressing, closing his

eyes as he savored it and the giblet gravy. "This is wonderful, Barbara."

"Thank you," she replied, with a big smile. "I love to cook."

"Me, too," Gwen added. "Barbara's teaching me how to do things properly."

"She's a quick study, too," Barbara replied, smiling at her daughter-in-law. "Her corn bread is wonderful, and I didn't teach her that . . . it's her own recipe. She's very talented."

"Thanks."

"What about this Fuentes character who side-swiped that car you were in?" he asked Gwen suddenly.

"Strange thing," she replied, tongue in cheek. "Fuentes seems to have gone missing. Nobody's seen him since the wreck."

"How very odd," the general remarked.

"Isn't it?"

"How about the young man who was driving you?" he added as he dipped his fork into potato salad.

"He's out of the hospital and back at work," Gwen said warmly. "He's going to be fine, thank goodness."

"I'm glad about that." He glanced across the table at Rick. "I understand that your father has left Mexico."

Rick smiled. "Yes, I did hear about that."

"So things are going to heat up in Barrera

very soon, I would expect," the general added.

Rick nodded. "Very soon."

"No more talk of revolution," Barbara said firmly. She got to her feet with a big grin. "I have a surprise."

She went into the kitchen and came back in with a huge coconut cream pie. She put it on the table.

"Is that . . . ?"

"Coconut cream." Barbara nodded. "I heard that it's someone's favorite."

"Mine!" General Cassaway said. "Thanks!"

"My pleasure." She cut it into slices and put one on a saucer for him. "If you still have room after all that turkey and dressing . . ."

"I'll make room," he said with such fervor that everyone laughed.

The general stayed for two days. Rick and Gwen and Barbara drove him around Jacobsville and introduced him to people. He fit in as if he'd been born there. He was coming back for Christmas, he assured them. He had to do a vanishing act to get out of all those holiday parties in Washington, D.C.

Rick heard from his father, too. The mercenaries had landed in a country friendly to Machado, near the border of Barrera, and they were massing for an attack. Machado told Rick not to worry, he was certain of victory. But just in case, he wanted Rick to know that the high point of his life so far had been meeting his own son. Rick had been over-whelmed with that statement. He told Gwen later that it had meant more to him than anything. Well, anything except marrying her, of course.

They moved back into her apartment, because it was closer to their jobs, leaving Rick's vacant for the moment.

She went home early one Friday night and when Rick walked in the door, he found her standing by the sofa wearing a negligee set that sent his heart racing like a bass drum.

"Here I was trying on my new outfit and there you are, home early. What perfect timing!" she purred, and moved toward him with her hair long and soft around her shoulders, her arms lifting to envelope him hungrily.

He barely got the door closed in time, before they wound up in a feverish tangle on the carpet . . . .

CHAPTER 11

➤———◄

"Your ribs," Rick gasped.

"Are fine," Gwen whispered, lifting to the slow, hard rhythm. Her eyes rolled back in her head at the overwhelming wave of pleasure that accompanied the movements. "Oh, my gosh!" she groaned, shivering.

"It just gets better . . . and better," he bit off.

"Yes . . . !" A high-pitched little cry escaped her tight throat. She opened her eyes wide as he began to shudder and she watched him. His body rippled in the throes of ecstasy. He closed his eyes and groaned helplessly as he arched up and gave himself to the pleasure.

Watching him set her own body on fire. She moved involuntarily, lifting, lifting, tightening as she felt the pleasure grow and grow and grow, like a volcano throwing out rocks and flame before it suddenly exploded and sent fiery rain into the sky. She was like the volcano, echoing its explosions, feeling her body burn and flame and consume itself in the endless fires of passion.

She couldn't stop moving, even when the

pinnacle was reached and she was falling from the hot peak, down into the warm ashes.

"No," she choked. "No . . . it's too soon . . . !"

"Shhhhh," he whispered at her ear. "I won't stop until you ask me to." He brushed her mouth with his and moved back into a slow, deep rhythm that very quickly brought her from one peak to an even higher one.

He lifted his head and looked down at her pretty pink breasts, hard-tipped and thrusting as she lifted to him, her flat belly reaching up to tempt his to lie on it, press it into the soft carpet as the rhythm grew suddenly quick and hard and urgent.

"Now, now, now," she moaned helplessly, shivering as the pleasure began to grow beyond anything she'd experienced before in his arms. "Oh, please, now!"

He pushed down, hard, and felt her ripple around him, a flutter of motion that sent him careening off the edge into space. He cried out, his body contracting as he tried to get even closer.

They shuddered and shuddered together, until the pleasure finally began to seep into manageable levels. He collapsed on her, his body heavy and hard and hot, and she held him while they started to breathe normally again.

"That was incredible," she whispered into his throat.

"I thought we'd already found the limit," he whispered back. "But apparently, we hadn't." He laughed weakly. He lifted his head. "Your rib," he said suddenly.

"It's fine," she assured him. "I wouldn't have felt it if it wasn't fine," she added with a becoming flush. She searched his dark eyes. "You're just awesome."

He grinned. "So are you." He lifted an eyebrow. "I hope you plan to make a habit of meeting me at the door in a see-through pink negligee. Because I have to tell you, I really like it."

She laughed softly. "It was impromptu. I was trying it on and I heard your key in the door. The rest is history."

He kissed her softly. "History indeed."

He started to lift away and she grimaced.

"Sorry," he said, and moved more gently. "We went at it a little too hard."

"No, we didn't," she denied, smiling even through the discomfort.

He led her into the bedroom and tucked them both into bed, leaving the clothes where they'd been strewn.

"We haven't had supper," she protested.

"We had dessert. Supper can wait." He pulled her into his arms and turned out the light. And they slept until morning.

Christmas Day brought a huge meal, the whole family except for General Machado, and holiday music around the Christmas tree in the living room of Barbara's house. Rick and Gwen had bid on the nearby house and the family selling it accepted. They were signing the papers the following month. It was an exciting time.

Barbara and General Gene Cassaway were getting along from time to time, but with minor and unexpected explosions every few hours. The general was very opinionated, it seemed, and he had very definite ideas on certain methods of cooking. Considering that he'd only started being a chef five years before, and Barbara had been doing it for years, they were bound to clash. And they did. The more they discussed recipes, the louder the arguments became.

Gwen had resigned her federal job, with her father's blessing, and was now working full-time as a detective on Rick's squad at San Antonio P.D.

Her fledgling efforts had resulted in murder charges against Mickey Dunagan, the man arrested but not convicted on assault charges concerning a college coed. He was also the subject of another investigation on a similar cold case, in which charges were pending. He'd been seen at the most recent victim's apartment before her death in San Antonio.

Faced with ironclad evidence of his guilt, a partial fingerprint and conclusive DNA matching fluids found on the victim's body, he'd confessed. A public defender had tried to argue that the Miranda rights hadn't been read, but the prisoner himself had assured his legal counsel that he'd been read them, and that he stood on his confession. He'd started crying. He hadn't meant to hurt any of them, but they were so pretty and he could never even get a girl to go out with him. He'd killed that other girl, too, because she'd made fun of him and laughed.

This girl he'd just killed, she'd been kind. He didn't care if he went to prison, he told Gwen. He didn't want to hurt anybody else.

She'd handed him over to the prosecutor's office with a sad smile. A murderer with a conscience. How unusual. But it didn't bring the dead women back. On the other hand, the cold case squad was feeling a sense of satisfaction. They owed Gwen a nice dinner, they told her, and would deliver any time she asked. She also spoke with the parents of the dead women, and gave them some consolation, in the fact that the killer would be brought to justice and, most likely, without a long and painful trial that would only bring back horrible memories of the tragedies.

The San Antonio patrolman, Sims, who'd gone on stakeout with Rick and Gwen, had been resigned from the force suddenly, with no reason given. Nobody in the department knew what had happened.

Patrolman Ames in Jacobsville was happily back on the job and with no apparent ill effects.

Down in Barrera, there were rumors of an

invasion. It was all over the news. General Cassaway, when asked about the truth of those rumors, just smiled.

Gwen handed Rick a wrapped gift and waited patiently for him to open it.

He looked inside and then back at her with wonder. "How did you know . . . ?"

She grinned and nodded toward Barbara, who laughed.

"Thanks!" he said, pulling out a DVD of an important United States vs. Mexico soccer match that he'd had to miss because of work. "I'll really enjoy it."

"I know you saw the results, but it was a great game," Gwen said.

"Here. Open yours," he said, and handed her a small present.

She pulled it open. It was a jeweler's box. She pulled the lid up and there was a small, beautiful diamond ring.

He pulled it out and slid it onto her finger. "I thought you should have one. It isn't the biggest around, but it's given with my whole heart."

He kissed it. She burst into tears and hugged him close. "I wouldn't care if it was a cigar band," she said.

"I know. That's why I wanted you to have it."

"Sweet man," she murmured.

He sighed. "Happy man," he added, kissing her hair.

She looked up at him with eyes full of love. "You know," she said, glancing toward her mother and General Cassaway, who were looking at recipe books they'd given each other, "I think this is the best Christmas of my life."

"I know it's the best of mine," he replied. "And only the first of many."

"Yes," she said, smiling from ear to ear as she touched his cheek with her fingertips. "The first of many. Merry Christmas."

He kissed her. "Merry Christmas."

The sudden buzz of his cell phone interrupted them. He reached into his pocket with a grimace. It was probably a case and he'd have to go to San Antonio on Christmas Day . . . .

He looked at the number. It was an odd sort of number. . . .

"Hello?" he said.

"Feliz Navidad," a deep voice sang, "Feliz Navidad, Feliz Navidad, something-somethingy felicidad!"

"You forgot the words?" Rick laughed, delighted. "Shame! It's '*Feliz Navidad, próspero año y felicidad*,' " he added smugly.

"Yes, shame, but I am very busy and my mind is on other things. Happy Christmas, my son."

"Happy Christmas to you, Dad," he said, glowing because his father had taken time out of a revolution to wish him well.

"Things are going fine here. Perhaps soon you

and your lovely wife will come to visit me, and I will send a plane for you."

"That would be nice," Rick said. He mouthed "Dad" to Gwen, who grinned.

"Meanwhile, be a good boy and Santa Claus will send you something very nice in the near future."

"I didn't get you anything," Rick said with sadness.

There was a deep chuckle. "You did. The hope of grandchildren. That is a gift beyond measure."

"I'll do my best," Rick replied, tongue in cheek.

There was an interruption. "Yes, I will be right there. Sorry. I have to go. Wish me luck."

"You know I do."

"And Happy Christmas, my son."

"Happy Christmas."

He hung up.

"That was a very nice surprise," Rick said.

She smiled. "Yes."

"It's not a simple recipe," the general was growling. "Nobody can make that right! It's a stupid recipe, it curdles every time!"

"It's not stupid, and yes, you can," Barbara growled back.

"I'm telling you, it's impossible! I know, I've tried!"

"Oh, for heaven's sake! Come on in here and I'll show you. It's not hard!"

"That's what you think!"

"Stop growling. It's Christmas."

The general made a face. "All right, damn it."

"Gene!"

He sighed. "Darn it."

"Much better," she said with a grin.

"I won't be reformed by a cook," he informed her. "And just in case you didn't notice, I'm head of the CIA!"

"In this house, you're an apprentice chef. Now stop muttering and come on. This is one of the easiest sauces in the world, and you won't curdle it if you'll just pay attention."

The general was still muttering as he followed Barbara into the kitchen. There was a loud rattle of pots and pans and the opening of the fridge. Voices murmured.

Rick pulled Gwen into his arms and kissed her hungrily. "I love you."

"I love you, too."

"See? I told you! That's curdling!"

"It's not curdling, it's reducing!"

"Damn it, you put the butter in too soon!" the general was raging.

"I did not!"

Rick rolled his eyes. "Do you think you could do something about your father?"

"If you'll do something about your mother," she returned with a grin.

"I'm not raising the heat. That book is wrong!" the general snapped.

Rick looked at Gwen. Gwen looked at Rick. In

the kitchen, the voices were growing louder. Without a word, they went to the front door, opened it and ran for their car.

Rick was laughing. "They won't even miss us," he said as he started the vehicle. "And maybe if they're left alone, they'll make peace."

"You think?" she teased.

He drove off to the house they were buying, cut off the engine and stared at it.

"We're going to be very happy here," Gwen said, sighing. "I'll make a garden and your mother can teach me how to can."

"Yes." He pulled her close. "If she and your father don't kill each other," he added.

"They'll have to learn to get along."

"Ha!"

The phone rang. Rick opened it. "Hello?"

"Could you come home for a minute?" Barbara asked.

"Sure. If it's safe," he teased. "What do you need?"

"Well, we could use a little help in the kitchen."

"Making the sauce?"

"Getting hollandaise sauce out of hair. And curtains. And cabinets. And on walls . . ."

"Mom!" he exclaimed. "What happened?"

"He thought I was making it wrong and I thought he was making it wrong, and, well, we sort of, uh, tossed the pan up."

"Are you okay?"

"Actually, you know, I think he was right. It tastes pretty good with less salt."

"I see."

"He's looking for another frying pan, so could you hurry?" she whispered, and then hung up.

"What's going on?" Gwen asked.

He grinned as he started the car. "War of the Worlds Part I. We get to help clean up the carnage in the kitchen."

"Excuse me?"

"They trashed the hollandaise sauce all over the kitchen."

"At least they're speaking," she pointed out.

He just shook his head. The general and his mother might eventually agree to a truce, but Rick had a feeling that it was going to be a long winter.

He pulled Gwen close and kissed the top of her head. He could manage anything, he thought, as long as he had her.

She sighed and closed her eyes. "Too many cooks spoil the broth?" she wondered aloud.

"I was thinking the same thing," he agreed. "Let's go referee."

"Done!"

They drove home through the colorful streets, with strings of red and blue and yellow and green lights and garlands of holly and fir. In the middle of the town square was a huge Christmas tree full of decorations, under which were wooden painted presents.

"One day," Rick said, "we'll bring our kids here when they light the tree."

She beamed. "Yes," she said, and it was a promise. "One day."

The tree grew smaller and smaller in the rearview mirror as they turned down the long road that led to Barbara's house. It was, Rick thought, truly the best Christmas of his life. He looked down at Gwen, and he saw in her eyes that she was thinking the very same thing.

Two lonely people, who found in each other the answer to a dream.

ABOUT THE AUTHOR

The prolific author of more than one hundred books, Diana Palmer got her start as a newspaper reporter. A multi-*New York Times* and *USA TODAY* bestselling author and one of the top ten romance writers in America, she has a gift for telling the most sensual tales with charm and humor. Diana lives with her family in Cornelia, Georgia.

Center Point Publishing
600 Brooks Road ● PO Box 1
Thorndike ME 04986-0001 USA

(207) 568-3717

US & Canada:
1 800 929-9108
www.centerpointlargeprint.com